"You're a
falling f

Jenny gasped at the accusing
statement. "Really, this is . . . of all the silly,
egotistical . . ."

"Do you think I didn't notice what
happened when I kissed you the other
night?" Paul grinned at her discomfort.
"You practically melted into a puddle at my
feet."

"Melted!" she echoed unconvincingly.
"These fantasies of yours are very
entertaining, Paul Brant, but let me assure
you I could spend days—weeks—in your
presence without so much as a flutter of the
pulse!"

Paul threw back his head and laughed.
"You know, I'm inclined to take a remark
like that as a personal challenge. And," he
added, suddenly thoughtful, "it looks as if
we both have something to prove."

Emily Spenser admits she was envious when her husband sold his first mystery novel. So in 1982 she sat down and wrote *Chateau Villon* for Harlequin Romance and has been writing ever since. Now she and her husband share interesting careers that combine travel with creative work. They live in Sequim, Washington, and when they're not writing or taking trips to research backgrounds for future books, they can be found exploring the mountains and coastlines, clamming or trying to learn the game of golf.

Books by Emily Spenser

Where Eagles Soar

Emily Spenser

Harlequin Books

TORONTO • NEW YORK • LONDON
AMSTERDAM • PARIS • SYDNEY • HAMBURG
STOCKHOLM • ATHENS • TOKYO • MILAN

Original hardcover edition published in 1987
by Mills & Boon Limited

ISBN 0-373-02898-9

Harlequin Romance first edition March 1988

Printed in U.S.A.

CHAPTER ONE

WHAT a way to fly!

No question about it; this was the purest, the most exhilarating form of flight that man had yet devised.

Ah . . . The wind current was strengthening. Paul Conan Brant the Third zipped his tan windbreaker the rest of the way up, shifted his weight to the left, pulled up on the control bar, and the Eagle VI ultralight instantly changed course. Incredible! The mini-plane responded as if its wings were an extension of his own arms. Reaching out, he shut off the small engine mounted behind him, and the motor-driven plane reverted to a hang-glider. For a moment his ears still thrummed with the engine's mechanical chattering; then they cleared, and the singing of the wind in the wires and an occasional soft creak from the fabric-covered wings were all that could be heard.

Shoving the nose down sharply to hold on to his airspeed, he exulted in the sensation of soaring like a majestic bird, drifting in solitary, lordly command of earth and sky. And what a place to soar! His cool, green eyes glowed with pleasure as he looked down. Magnificent. Weird. Fantastic. How could you possibly describe the rock formations of the Chiricahua Mountains two thousand feet below?

But the scenery was a minor pleasure compared to

the knowledge that no one could intrude on his solitude. Far from conventional flight paths, and with no radio, there was no ground control barking at him, telling him what and what not to do. His lips curled into a faint smile. If they only knew where he was and had some way of contacting him, some desk-bound air traffic controller would be carping away at him right now, telling him to turn back, that it was illegal to fly into the Chiricahua National Monument's airspace.

He must have strayed into it all right, because the countryside below him was quickly turning into a maze of deep, plunging canyons, rearing precipices, and thousands of impossibly tall, slender rock columns eroded by the elements into an arid fantasy land like nothing else in the world. It was as if he were looking down on a stupendous cave with the roof removed, so that he could see the forest of thousand-foot-high stalagmites on its floor.

Or did he mean stalactites? The hell with it; it was really something to see!

Feeling his airspeed drop—the wind current must have diminished—he took his eyes off the landscape and flipped the engine switch on again. He hadn't the slightest desire to turn back. Not even if he was doing a little trespassing. No, up here, suspended in the fragile, open-framework pilot's seat of this simple craft he felt a measure of serenity—something he hadn't felt for a long time. Besides, he wanted to get a closer look at those astonishing piles of rock.

Adjusting his weight again and pushing down on the control bar, Paul tipped his ultralight into a dive to pick up speed and then racked it into a tight turn, hauling it around as hard as he could. He started to lean back and enjoy the lazy ride down when, without warning, the mini-plane shuddered, stalled, and twisted violently on to its back. He was stunned by the suddenness of it, his vision blurred, his equilibrium disorientated, as he tumbled upside down, hanging heavily against the restraints. Then, just as suddenly, the Eagle VI stopped dead for a breathless second, etched like a photograph against the turquoise sky, and dropped like a stone towards the ground.

With a relieved outrush of breath Paul tightened his fingers on the control bar. Pulling out of vertical dives was child's play. He had been doing that since he'd learned to fly at sixteen. He pulled the nose up with a smooth, co-ordinated movement, but to his amazement the ultralight stalled, tilted crazily, and then flipped over again! What in the hell was going on?

Again the Eagle VI tumbled out of control for a few wild seconds, and then again it plunged into a vertical, screaming dive. This time the ground was terrifyingly closer.

At least it should have been terrifying. Any normal person would have panicked. Paul didn't. He wasn't even frightened, in any ordinary sense of the word. Even as he plummeted out of control he was aware of little more than a cool detachment, a remote interest, as if this were all happening to someone else. Good God, was he really so world-weary, so jaded, that he could be moments from death and not feel anything at all? No, that wasn't quite true. He felt something all right: curiosity about why this thing seemd to be defying every principle of aerodynamics he knew. His brain searched through its stored data as dispassionately as a computer accessing its data banks.

He hit on it in a few seconds, while impassively watching the sun-baked rock spires swarm up towards him. Of course! It was the G-loading. When he had racked the craft into that tight turn, it must have reached its critical angle more quickly than the conventional aircraft he was used to. So it stalled at a speed well above the normal one-G stalling speed. And because he was in a turn, the simultaneous loss of lift and increase in drag had tugged it around, flipping it on to its back and whirling it into a dive. Instead of pulling up, he should have lowered the nose to unstall the thing.

Driven more by intellectual curiosity than self-preservation, he tried the experiment and pressed *down* on the control bar. It worked. With a sluggish whoof the ultralight slowed and began to pull tremblingly out of the dive. Too late, though, he thought with a sort of distant sadness; too late to do any good.

He was right. As if he were watching an absorbing movie, he looked on as the left wing scraped against the side of a massive stone column and then crumpled and tore away. The Eagle VI sagged and spun crazily to bounce against another rock wall, and then still another, sinking towards the rugged canyon floor all the time.

So this was how it was going to end. Well, why not? He had challenged death a hundred times—on Everest, in the Atlantic, behind the wheel of the Maserati—and won. He had to lose some time; he'd always known that. But somehow, for it to happen here, in this inaccessible corner of Arizona that no one had ever heard of, sitting helplessly in a jokelike contraption of fabric and balsa wood . . .

He must have hit his head. There wasn't any pain, but his thoughts suddenly seemed to scatter and fly away, and blackness closed in at the edges of his vision. Only at the centre could he see clearly, as if he were looking down a long tunnel. Then that too began to waver, like a candle in the breeze. But only for a moment, before the candle was snuffed soundlessly out and there was nothing but darkness.

He was freezing. And he didn't seem to be able to open his eyes.

Was he paralysed? Dead? No, not dead; the rocks digging into his back hurt too much for him to be dead. He tried to shift his body, and the unexpected explosion of pain made him gasp. But at least his eyes flew open. Something worked.

They didn't do him much good. It was pitch-dark. For a while he lay still, afraid to move again, his mind empty of everything except the cold, and then, gingerly, he moved his left arm. It made him wince, but he knew it wasn't broken, just bruised. Cautiously, he tried out his other limbs. All responded, if weakly. The feel of gravelly sand against him puzzled him. Where was he?

There was something fluttering languidly against his face. He strained his eyes, trying to make it out in the frigid starlight. A shirt? A rag? Tired with the effort, he closed his eyes. My God, it was cold!

And all at once he remembered. He had crashed, and somehow come out of it in one piece. He opened his eyes again and reached up to push at the broken fabric-covered wing section obscuring his vision. Featherlight, it fell away easily. The torrent of stars that filled the black sky were as sharp as gems, as hard and cold as ice crystals—graphic reminders that hypothermia—heat loss—would finish him off if he didn't do something; tear fabric off the wings and wrap it around himself ... build a fire ... do anything but lie there waiting to die. All it took was initiative.

There were two problems. No doubt there were more, but two were all he could handle at the moment. The first was that it was peaceful, even beautiful, lying here, despite the cold. And the other was that if the key to survival really was his initiative—the intensity of his will to survive—then he was keyless. Survive for what? For whom? There was no work to return to, no career, nobody who really wanted or needed him. Hadn't he been flirting with death for years anyhow, and lately, to be honest, hadn't it got just a little flat?

How much simpler, how much easier it would be just to lie here ... quietly ... tranquilly ... and let it all go. He yawned, closed his eyes and nestled into the soft sand. What had made him think he was so uncomfortable, so cold? In fact, he was feeling downright contented; warm, calm, sleepy ... deliciously sleepy.

'Paul, Paul ... hang in there. I'm with you now. I'll soon have you safe.' Her voice was soft but insistent. 'Paul. Listen to me, Paul. Just hold on. Everything's all right now.' Semi-conscious, he fought her voice. She was trying to force him out of the dark void where he floated so effortlessly, and back into the world of people and of cold.

'We'll have you out in no time at all.' She was leaning over him now, holding his hand with one of hers and stroking his forehead, then his cheek, with the other. Her touch was harder to ignore—gentle, feminine, delicious. He managed to grin to himself; he'd taken a heck of a beating, but he was a long way from dead.

Slowly he became aware of other things—the sound of the plane's wreckage being dragged away, the harsh static of a short-wave radio, deep male voices saying things he couldn't make out. Someone had wrapped a blanket around him, put him on a stretcher.

She was speaking to him again.

'Paul? Paul? Can you hear me? I'm with you now. You'll soon be safe. All you have to do is hold on, don't give up, don't let go ...'

He puzzled over the concern in her voice. She was a stranger. He was sure she was a stranger. Wasn't she? Spurred by a growing curiosity, Paul fought his way out of the black void long enough to get his eyes opened. He could see her clearly in the harsh, white glare of artificial light. She was pretty . . . Somehow he'd known that from her voice. Not glamorous pretty but girl-next-door pretty; clean, and fresh, and outdoorsy. Her ash-brown hair was caught in a ponytail that fell over one shoulder and brushed against his forehead like silk, smooth and tantalising, when she leaned over him. Yes, he was definitely alive, all right!

He dragged his gaze from her hair to her face. She was smiling at him, but only with her mouth. Her blue-grey eyes mirrored nothing but anxiety for him, and he couldn't begin to figure out why. For he was right: he had never seen her before. With every passing second, though, with his eyes locked on hers, she grew more familiar . . . more precious.

Paul closed his eyes. The light hurt them and the strain of trying to think was too much for him.

'That's right, Paul,' she said soothingly. 'Relax, but don't let go.' She squeezed his hand. 'I'll stay with you, don't worry. We'll have you out in no time at all.'

He wished he had the energy to explain things. He didn't want out. He didn't want anything at all, only to lie there without moving and let the soft music of her voice flow over him. It flowed, but it also pulled, tugged, pushed, so that without meaning to he found himself listening, responding, unwillingly accepting the unwanted infusion of strength she offered him—strength enough indeed to hold on . . .

Jenny parked her battered Buick station wagon in the carport and switched off the headlights. Thank goodness she'd made it home without falling asleep behind the wheel. If not for that gallon of coffee consumed at the hospital while waiting to help reclaim the team's equipment—and, all right, to hear for sure that the pilot would make it—she would have had to sleep in her car in the hospital car park.

She glanced at the luminous green dial of her watch. No wonder she was tired! The plane hadn't been located until midnight, after ten gruelling hours of searching, and then it had taken another four and the efforts of seventeen people to complete the rescue operation. Eight men had been needed just to guide the stretcher down the steep trail leading out of Deming Canyon. But wilderness rescues required more than muscles and sure-footedness. The presence, voice, and touch of another caring human being could make the difference between life and death, and Jenny's job during the last few hours had been to be that human being, to stay by the side of the victim and keep alive the desire to live.

'The victim'. Who was she trying to kid? Five minutes after she had knelt by his side he'd become 'Paul', and no longer the anonymous, impersonal 'victim'. She folded her arms over the steering wheel and laid her head heavily on them. What had happened to her out there? What was it in the man's face that had so unexpectedly touched her in a way she'd never quite been touched before?

There was an obvious answer, but it missed the mark. No, it wasn't because he was so ruggedly handsome, or because the arrogance and confidence that stood out in every line of his face contrasted so

appealingly with that sensual mouth. And no, it
wasn't the way his thick, waving brown hair fell so
boyishly over his wide forehead. No, she had seen
handsome men before. There was something else, a
touching, indescribable look of vulnerability and
loneliness beneath the strong features, that came and
went as he slipped in and out of insensibility. She
could see him work to suppress it each time he drifted
towards consciousness. Just as Jenny herself had
become adept at hiding exactly those two painful
emotions.

But there had been more than that. When Paul's
deep-set green eyes had fluttered open, they had been
gentle and questioning, and had looked so deeply
inside her that they had seemed to sear a brand on
her soul.

A brand . . .! Jenny jerked her head up and shook it.
She must be more exhausted than she thought, to
allow her mind to go off rhapsodising over a man she
didn't even know. And when she thought about it,
her reaction infuriated her. Because what little she
did know about him, she most certainly didn't
approve of.

She ought to be despising—not mooning over—a
man stupid enough to fly an ultralight over the
rugged, unforgiving wilderness of the Chiricahuas. A
man whose childish 'pleasure cruise' had kept the
entire search-and-resuce team up all night, not to
mention the Chiricahua National Monument staff,
the Coronado National Forest rangers, the Sheriff's
department helicopter pilot . . . Honestly . . .

She got out of the car wearily, and went into the

second unit of the apartment house, then continued
to mutter to herself while she stripped off her dirt-
soiled shirt, her jeans, and her hiking boots. Because
of that thoughtless, devil-may-care pilot, she would
be lucky if she could keep from falling asleep right in
front of the customers at the bank tomorrow
morning. This morning, rather; she was due on the
job in two hours. Darn that man!

She fell on to the bed, determinedly thrusting all
thoughts of Paul from her mind, and very success-
fully, too—until she fell asleep ten seconds later.
Then his face appeared with such startling, smiling
clarity that she smiled in return and reached gently
out to touch it.

CHAPTER TWO

'PAUL CONAN BRANT III Leaves Hospital Today.'

Jenny took one look at the headline and tossed the *Cochise Bend Observer* back down on the end table in the employees' lounge. It had been a week since Brant's rescue, and still colour rose to her cheeks at the memory of her lunatic fantasies that night. Glad that no one else was sharing the lounge during her afternoon break, she walked to the coffee pot and poured herself a steadying cupful.

A look of vulnerability and loneliness . . . She cringed at the memory. True, she'd had no way of knowing at the time that a downed ultralight pilot by the name of Paul Brant was *the* Paul Conan Brant the Third, but that didn't excuse her incredible naïveté.

Paul Brant had first caught the public's attention a decade before when, at twenty-two, he decided to sail the Atlantic single-handed. True, it had been done before, but not in late November, in a slender, thirty-foot Swan ketch. As the pessimists had predicted, he was caught in a major storm, failed to show up on schedule in Plymouth, England, and was presumed drowned. Weeks later, he turned up, starving and thirsty, but very much alive, on the island of Graciosa in the Azores, where the storm had blown his tiny craft.

From that point on, it was one hair-raising exploit

after another, all duly reported in the Press. And since he was ruggedly handsome, rich, and aristocratic besides, he provided excellent copy of another sort: he quickly developed a discriminating taste for fast cars and beautiful women, not necessarily in that order. But nothing seemed to capture his attention for long, nothing seemed to hold him for more than a week or a month.

All in all, Jenny thought, a man like that was about as vulnerable as a Sherman tank! And as lonely as an Eastern potentate with a well-stocked harem. Reflectively, she stirred powdered cream into her coffee and sipped it. To be fair to herself, Cochise County, Arizona was a pretty unlikely spot for a jet-set adventurer to show up in, so she really couldn't be too hard on herself.

In the old Wild West days, it might have been a different story. Frontiersmen and fortune hunters had poured in by the thousands during the silver rush days of the 1880s, and the county became notorious for raucous towns like Tombstone and Cochise Bend, where the only law was the six-shooter. And if that weren't enough to make life hazardous, the brooding Chiricahua Mountains were near-impregnable Apache strongholds. Mounted on horseback, the Indians swooped devastatingly down on wagon trains, stage-coaches and ranches to pillage and burn, hoping to drive the never-ending hordes of white men back to wherever they were coming from—the east coast, Great Britain, Italy, Finland. Even Serbs, Croatians, and Montenegrins found their way to the mining fields.

But those feverish days were long gone, and so were most of the bawdy old towns. Cochise Bend was an exception, still there in the hollow between the red hills, right where it always had been, kept alive for a while by two big copper mines after the silver veins had run dry, and now a sleepy little town in the Arizona desert, decent, quiet, and unexceptional. And dull.

Having grown up there, Jenny could testify to that. With its 'nightlife' limited to one sixty-year-old movie theatre that was closed from Monday through Thursday, it was hardly the kind of place one would expect Paul Conan Brant or his like to surface. History buffs, bird-watchers, hikers, maybe, but not the swingers and the trend-setters. The pavements didn't literally roll up after dark but they might as well have, and people who needed more thrills moved to Tucson or Phoenix, or left Arizona altogether for California, their glittering neighbour to the west. Just as Jenny had planned to do . . . once.

Sometimes it was still hard to believe that when her father had died she had decided not to go off to Los Angeles with her mother and sister, but to stay. Still that was all beside the point. The important thing was to remember that she had made a fool of herself over Paul Brant, even if she was the only one who knew it. And if that was an indication of her ability to assess the male of the species, maybe it was a good thing she had dropped out of the game.

But dropping out of the game was one thing, controlling her feelings and her thoughts another, and there was no denying that Paul Brant had been strangely involved in both for a week now. Regardless of what she'd read about him, regardless of what she knew about the splashy, pointless way he lived, he had somehow stirred something in her. When his eyelids had fluttered open and he had looked at her with those transparently green eyes in the split second before that protective, arrogant veil slid down over them, she had trembled, actually trembled. She had more than trembled; she had felt as if ... almost as if ...

No, this was ridiculous! Pointless. Absolutely juvenile, and she would stop this minute! She washed out her ceramic mug, hung it on a hook in the cupboard and stepped firmly from the lounge, Paul Conan Brant resolutely pushed from her mind. How silly to waste her break thinking about him, as if break time didn't pass all too quickly, anyway. If only work time did the same. Still, it was hard to complain. Her bank teller's job was one routine after another, but Mr Rayburn thoroughly approved of and supported her membership in the county's volunteer search-and-rescue team. And that provided enough excitement for anyone. Sometimes more than enough, she added wryly.

She opened the grille at her work station just in time to see Ed Burnaby shuffle noisily through the bank's heavy glass doors. Jenny would have known the thin, stoop-shouldered old man with her eyes closed. Ed literally jingled. Kim, the other teller, was busy with Mrs Pursall, who drove all the way in from Nicksville every week to do her banking business, so

Ed was all hers, a prospect that appeared to delight him.

'Well, hello there, young lady,' the old man sang, plunking several small, grimy sacks of coins on the counter. 'How's my favourite banker?'

Ed owned the coin-operated laundry in town and it was one of Jenny's less-liked tasks to count all the dimes and quarters he brought in twice a week for deposit. Once, she had suggested to him how much easier it would be if he rolled his own coins, and she had offered to give him a supply of wrappers. His face had fallen pathetically at the idea, and she had never had the heart to mention it again. In a town like Cochise Bend there was more to banking than money.

'Nice weather,' Ed drawled happily, searching for—and finding—still more coins in his pockets, 'but I hear we might get a hard freeze tonight. What do you think?'

'Let's hope not,' Jenny said, opening the first sack and turning it on to the counter. 'It's March already.'

'That don't matter none.' The old man snorted with laughter. 'Why, the nearest I ever come to freezing to death was on the road between here and Bisbee, and that was on the thirtieth of *July*! That was in 'thirty-five, when we had that terrific hailstorm, the one that killed my brother Albert's bull. No, wait, it must have been 'thirty-six, because he didn't get that bull till . . .'

If Jenny hadn't always been in the awkward position of counting stacks of coins, she would have enjoyed Ed's stories a lot more. As it was, it was a strain to keep the figures straight while smiling and nodding at reasonably appropriate moments. Still, it helped pass the time, and so far she'd never made a mistake.

Until today. When the bank door opened again as she started on the second bag, everything dropped out of her mind—quarters, dimes, Albert's bull, everything. The tall, wide-shouldered figure that strode so confidently and casually over the gleaming wooden floor seemed to make not only her mind stop, but her heart as well. Then, with a lurch, as if someone had grabbed and twisted it, it started again, hammering so loudly that everyone in the bank must have heard it.

Quickly, before Paul Brant could spot her, she bent her head over the coin stacks, letting her shoulder-length hair obscure her face.

Not that she had too much to worry about, she reminded herself gratefully. People in the throes of hypothermia are usually dazed, and it was highly unlikely he would recognise anyone from the team. And of course it was positively impossible—thank goodness—for him to know what had been going on in her mind. Still, she wasn't about to take any chances.

Only why hadn't he picked the First Union Bank across the street to cash a cheque in, she wondered irritably, instead of walking in here and rattling her like this? And what was he doing in a bank, anyway, almost within minutes of getting out of the hospital? No doubt he wanted to get enough money to make a quick escape from what he probably thought of as a poky little backwater of a town. If he bothered to think of it at all, that is.

Jenny blinked with surprise at the irrational indignation that boiled up so strongly she could feel it like a tight little ball at the base of her throat. Why in the world should she be angry with him for wanting to get out of Cochise Bend? Why shouldn't he? And what did it matter to her? Bewildered, she bent even closer to the coins. One thing she knew: she wasn't picking up her head until Kim finished with Mrs Pursall, took him as a customer, and sent him back out into Copper Street with his money. Ed Burnaby might have a longer visit than even he had in mind.

Ten minutes later, while she was still struggling confusedly with the second sack of coins and Ed was telling her about the time his cousin Pearl had accidentally left a sheep in the laundry over the weekend, she heard the words she'd been longing for.

'Goodbye now, Mrs Pursall, and have a nice week.'

Despite the crick in her neck, Jenny kept her head down. Was he still even there? Maybe the wait had been too long and he had gone across the street.

He was there all right. She knew that when she heard Kim catch her breath and tune her normally crisp and businesslike voice down two octaves, to something that sounded like a saxophone in heat. 'I can help you over here, sir,' she purred. 'I'll be very glad to help you. Very glad.'

Boy, if that was the way strange women typically responded to the man, Jenny mused, her head still averted, Paul Brant must have an ego the size of a football field! How perfectly silly of Kim to turn into quivering jelly just because . . . A warm spot tingled at the back of Jenny's neck. She was hardly in a position to make judgements.

'No thanks.' His voice was low and resonant, as confident as if he owned the bank. 'I'm waiting to talk to Miss Roberts.'

Jenny straightened up with a jerk and found him looking not at Kim, but gazing straight at her with those clear, riveting green eyes. When he caught her eyes and held them—she could no more break away than she could stop her heartbeat—the firm, sensual lines of his mouth slowly relaxed into a smile.

Regarding him as coolly and steadily as she could, despite the fact that her heart was in her throat, she said, 'I'm afraid I'll be a while yet.' She gestured to Ed. 'I'm sure Miss Conley will——'

'Oh, I can wait.'

Dazedly aware that Paul's cool, challenging eyes continued to assess her with embarrassing frankness, she forced her attention back to her customer.

'Well, thank you now, Jenny,' Ed said when she finally handed him his receipt. He glanced slyly over his shoulder to peep at the stranger waiting to speak to his favourite teller, and then turned back to her with the closest thing to a leer she had ever seen on his face. 'Well, now, it's about time you got yourself a new boyfriend,' he said in a stage whisper that could be heard in every corner of the room. 'Pretty girl like you.'

The old man turned, winked broadly at Paul, and

ambled contentedly away.

If there had been a hole within reach, Jenny would have crawled gratefully into it and never come up. Instead, all she could do was hope her cheeks weren't as pink as they felt, and smile apologetically when Paul came up to the counter. 'I'm sorry about that, Mr Brant.'

'Mr Brant?' he said, laughing engagingly. 'The last time I remember those gorgeous grey eyes gazing into mine it was "Paul".'

'Really, Mr Brant——'

'And there's no need to apologise about the old fellow. He did me a favour. Now that I know there's no fiancé in the background, I can ask you to dinner tonight with a clear conscience.' He put a corduroy-covered elbow on the table and leaned casually closer. 'What time shall I pick you up?'

Jenny restrained a wild impulse to turn around and run. 'D-dinner?'

'I'd say it's the least I can do.'

'Well ... um ...' Prepared to hear a short, awkward speech—rescued people did occasionally look up team members to thank them in person—she had been caught completely off guard, and she knew it showed.

'Dinner,' he repeated blandly. 'I assume that's what it's called in Cochise Bend? And don't even think about saying no. I don't take "nos" for answers.'

'Really, that's completely unnecessary,' she responded, bridling at the amusement in his eyes. Not that she could blame him, considering the idiotic way she'd been acting. She needed to pull herself together, and fast. 'I was simply doing my job,' she said with a semblance of composure. 'If you'd like to do something in the way of appreciation, our team can always use donations for new equipment.'

He grinned. 'I just came from dropping a cheque off at the Sheriff's department.' His grin turned wry. 'And paying a rather hefty fine,' he added, before his voice took on an abrupt, no-nonsense ring. 'What time do you get off work? Five?'

Jenny balked instinctively at his imperious manner. Her chin went firmly up and she very nearly told him just what she thought of him, but she couldn't help being aware that the rest of the bank staff—with the exception of Mr Rayburn in his office, thank heavens—were eavesdropping unabashedly. Besides, there was something in the way Paul was regarding her that made her think better of it. She doubted very much that she would come out ahead in a naked contest of wills.

'Well . . . yes,' she finally said tersely, hoping her cold tone would discourage him.

It didn't. He found it funny, which was even worse.

'Good. A highly intelligent answer.' He bit back a grin. 'See you at five.'

From the moment he strode out, Jenny couldn't decide which was worse; the thought of the upcoming dinner with Paul Brant—*Paul Brant!*—or the salivating interest of her co-workers in this extremely unexpected turn of events.

The door had barely closed behind him when

Kim, with undisguised envy all over her face, exclaimed, 'Jenny, you've *got* to go home and change into something less dowdy!' She pointed a disdainful finger at Jenny's green cotton blouse and straight skirt. 'You can't go out in that—with *him!*'

Milly, the loan officer, scurried avidly over. 'I couldn't help overhearing. I'm sure Mr Rayburn will give you the time off to go home and change. I mean, this is a special event!'

What is? Jenny was tempted to ask—that Paul Conan Brant the Third had condescendingly asked a small-town nobody to dinner? Or that Jenny Roberts had a date?

She shook her head firmly. 'I wouldn't dream of imposing on Mr Rayburn for something so insignificant,' she said pointedly, reading in their eyes the answer to a question that was bothering her. Just when had the staff and the town—Ed Burnaby was the town's weathercock for local opinion—begun thinking of her as spinster material? Not that it mattered. Or so she told herself, returning serenely to work. The fact that she couldn't put together two rational thoughts in a row, and that the ninety minutes until five o'clock seemed like ninety hours, was nobody's business but hers.

Paul was waiting for her outside the employees' entrance, and Jenny noticed at once that *he* had used the time to change clothes. She was immensely flattered, and more flustered than ever. Dressed in an off-white, linen bush jacket, a crisp, open-necked shirt, and tan trousers, he was positively dashing. More than that, his clothes, his posture, everything about him, radiated an almost visible sense of casual sophistication—and wealth. It was strange; she had never come into contact with such a quality before—she hadn't even known it existed—and yet it was unmistakable.

His arms folded, he was leaning against a Porsche, more relaxed and confident than anyone had a right to look. When he spotted her, he straightened and smiled.

Jenny returned the smile, her eyes drifting to the sports car. Her stomach was fluttery to begin with, without him driving a car that looked as if it were violating the speed limit standing still. She wondered if she even had the courage to get into it.

He moved to open the passenger door. Misinterpreting her glance at the car, he asked with a smile, 'Like sports cars?'

'No. Not really.'

It was the first time she had seen him taken even slightly aback. He cocked his head, raised a heavy, dark eyebrow, and shut her door.

Once inside, Jenny found a fresh reason to dislike the car. The bucket seats and narrow interior forced a closeness on them whether she liked it or not. And since she was already far too aware of him physically, she didn't like it one bit. She shifted uneasily.

'Will you relax a little if I promise not to speed?' he drawled, noting her unease and again jumping to the wrong conclusion, but this time to her relief.

She nodded warmly.

With a somewhat bemused expression, he started

the engine and rolled slowly out of the car park on to Arroyo Street.

'I was thinking about the Copper King Hotel,' he said, reaching the Main Street intersection. 'Does that sound all right to you?'

The hotel, built at the turn of the century, during Cochise Bend's heyday, was still the town's showpiece and its best dining spot. Paul Brant had done his homework. The idea should have pleased her—so why was she vaguely panicked by it? Still feeling ridiculously tongue-tied, she again nodded.

The ride, fortunately, was brief. It would have been briefer still had Paul not driven at a speed so excruciatingly slow that the Porsche must have blushed with embarrassment. Walking up the horseshoe-shaped portico stairs of the hotel with him, Jenny searched for something innocuous to say to break the increasingly awkward silence.

Paul beat her to it.

'How about a drink first?' he asked, gesturing to the swinging doors of the Ocotillo Bar that opened off the lobby.

She nodded willingly.

He stopped her with a touch on the arm. 'Jenny, you do speak, don't you? I'm sure I remember you speaking.'

She laughed. 'A drink sounds nice.'

But once inside, she blanched and gulped. Directly in front of them, above the long, old-fashioned bar of dark, gleaming wood, hung a huge painting of a very naked, extremely friendly-looking woman that dated back to lustier days when the Ocotillo was more dance-hall saloon than bar, and the upstairs rooms of the Copper King didn't cater to the family trade. Her embarrassment took her by surprise. She had seen the painting before—everybody in Cochise Bend had—and her reaction had been the same as everyone else's: the Naked Lady was a part of the town's rollicking history and, in her place there over the bar, she was a lively, even funny reminder of the wild, woolly old days.

Well, it didn't seem so funny now; the Naked Lady was suddenly mortifyingly erotic, oozing sex and suggestiveness from every exuberantly painted inch of steamy, pink flesh. Damn Paul Brant and that electric aura of sensuality that seemed to be a part of him! With him around, one of Uncle Gil's paint-by-number flower pictures would probably make her think sexy thoughts!

The focus of her unjustified irritation was busy taking in her reaction, looking from Jenny to the picture and back again, his head tilted to one side. He was close to laughing at her, she could see that, but she could also see that he was determined to do whatever he had to do to make the dinner pleasant for her.

'You know, it's a little stuffy in here,' he said politely enough, but barely managing to suppress his smile. 'I don't know about you, but I could use some fresh air. Aren't there some tables outside?' Without waiting for her to answer he led her out on to the adjoining patio.

He left her seated at the one white, wrought-iron table still touched by the fading sunshine, and went back into the bar to get their drinks. Jenny wouldn't have blamed him if he had lingered to have a quick one. First she'd been frightened by his car, and now she looked like the world's worst prude. And she hadn't been exactly a sparkling conversationalist so far. By now he had to be regretting his impulsive generosity and wondering how he was going to make it through the evening!

CHAPTER THREE

His speedy return from the bar spoke well of his fortitude if nothing else. And he hadn't even bought himself a double, Jenny thought wryly, thanking him for the glass of Chenin Blanc he put in front of her.

Taking the chair across from her, he crossed one long leg over the other, took a swallow of his whisky and soda, and smiled ruefully at her.

'Tell me, do you always chatter this much, or are you just particularly loquacious tonight?'

Jenny couldn't help laughing. 'I'm sorry.' She nervously twisted her glass on its green cardboard coaster. 'I guess your invitation was so unexpected that I'm a bit at a loss for words. Frankly, I assumed you'd be out of Cochise Bend—and Arizona—the minute they let you out of bed.'

To her surprise, Paul's jaw tightened, and for the first time his normally cool green eyes glinted with anger.

'I'm well aware that I have a reputation for being reckless—and I'd have a hard time refuting it, considering that mishap last week——' He paused, and when he continued, his voice had a steely ring she hadn't heard before. 'But I'm not sure I appreciate being thought of as someone who'd leave without bothering to say thanks.'

'But I didn't mean that at all,' Jenny said truthfully, astonished that he could describe a hair-raising brush with death, which had put him in the hospital for a week, as a 'mishap'. 'All I meant was that I can't imagine your finding much to interest you around here. This is a pretty quiet corner of the world. And just a simple letter of thanks would have been much appreciated.'

His annoyance faded as quickly as it came. 'Is that what your team usually gets—a letter?'

'Oh, it varies,' she replied, relieved at the chance to move the conversation from a personal level. 'Sometimes people express their appreciation with a note or a donation; sometimes we're thanked in person——' She smiled. 'And sometimes we're not thanked at all.'

'Doesn't it make you angry when that happens? They told me at the hospital that you're all volunteers; you don't get paid.'

She sipped her wine and shrugged. 'Gratitude isn't why I do it. And I certainly wouldn't do it for money.'

He eyed her over his Scotch. 'All right, I'm game; why do you do it? It's got to be hard, and you must see some pretty unpleasant sights. How did you get into it, anyway?'

She returned his steady, interested gaze, and to her own astonishment, actually came close to telling him, or trying to. But that would be something she'd never talked about with anyone, and probably never would; it was too deep, too much a part of her, and it hurt too much. Still, how curious that it should be this devil-may-care stranger—with whom she had nothing at all in common, whom she would never see again, and who probably wouldn't even remember her next week—that had almost brought it out of her.

'There are plenty of reasons,' she said lightly. 'Lots of fresh air, for instance, and it certainly makes a change from the bank.' She finished the Chenin Blanc. 'This wine has definitely whetted my appetite!'

Paul smiled enigmatically at her, not in the least taken in by her evasion. 'I guess that means you're still not quite willing to talk, but you're willing to eat.' He drained his glass. 'All right, let's eat, then.'

In the dining-room, he looked quickly over the menu and ordered for both of them: veal mornay with fresh asparagus, and a bottle of Pouilly-Fuissé. With a flash of irritation, Jenny very nearly told him she was quite capable of deciding on her own what she wanted, but she thought better of it and held her tongue. For one thing, she would never be seeing him again, so why make a scene? For another, he probably wouldn't even know what she was upset about; his arrogance fitted him like a custom-tailored suit. He was probably so used to females turning to jelly in his presence that he'd long ago given up believing they could think for themselves.

And for another, she admitted to herself, she was looking forward to the veal mornay. She had eaten at the Copper King a few times before—but she'd always been limited to the salisbury steak or the pasta. And the house wines. She had always wondered what kind of person could afford to order the Pouilly-Fuissé, which cost almost a full day's salary at the bank. Well, she was finding out.

'Will you think I'm being patronising if say that I'm surprised at how elegant this place is?' Paul said as the waitress left with the order.

'Yes,' Jenny retorted lightly, 'but since it's a compliment to Cochise Bend, you're forgiven.'

She glanced around at the dark blue walls with their white wainscoting, the massive antique sideboards, the stained glass windows ... The room reeked of the past; a very lush, opulent past. Most of the light came from ornate hurricane lamps that bathed the old wooden furniture with a soft, rich light. It was quiet too; except for two whispering men in a far corner who looked like lonely visiting salesmen, they had the room to themselves.

'I like to imagine what this must have looked like at the turn of the century,' Jenny said. 'The women would have been in those gorgeous off-the-shoulder gowns with——' She glanced embarrassedly down at her green skirt and blouse she had been wearing all day. 'I'm sorry I'm not dressed for the occasion. I wish I was wearing something nicer.'

It was the closest thing to an honest personal statement she had made all evening, and she felt better for it right away, but she spoiled it with her next sentence. 'I was so tied up at work, there just wasn't any chance to change.'

She could have kicked herself for that. In the first place it wasn't true, and she prided herself on being honest. And in the second place, why was she trying to convince him that this dinner date was important to her when it wasn't? Or was it? No, she told herself, it wasn't. After all, she *could* have gone home and changed, but had chosen to wear the simple outfit she had put on for work, so how important could it be?

On the other hand, since she was being so honest, why had her heart been skittering along at twice its normal rate ever since he'd walked into the bank that afternoon? Ever since he had opened his eyes and looked dazedly at her that night in the Chiricahuas, if she wanted to be *really* honest. No, the only thing she could say with certainty was that every time Paul Brant came near her, she got very confused indeed about what she thought. Or felt.

'Well, I'll let it pass, even if this is a pretty important occasion,' he joked, grimacing. 'My first non-hospital food in a week. And I hope you won't take it as an insult to the town if I tell you the Cochise Hospital isn't too big on veal mornay.' He frowned, as if considering something weighty. 'Not too bad on gruel and porridge, though.'

She laughed, and while he took an evaluative taste of the wine that had been brought to the table by a respectful wine steward, she took advantage of the opportunity to study his face for signs of last week's accident. They were few: his tan was slightly faded, and his face was a bit drawn, as if he had lost a pound or two, but if anything it made him look even more handsome, like a tragic matinée idol of fifty years ago. He had been devilishly lucky. And from out of nowhere an old saying popped into her mind: 'The devil takes care of his own.'

Now where had that come from? And what was it supposed to mean? Was it a warning to herself, or what? It was bad enough that *he* confused her; she had better stop doing it to herself. This was all very——

'The wine's not bad,' Paul said, cutting into her thoughts. He filled her glass, lifted it up into her hand, and raised his own glass. 'Thanks for seeing me through up there.'

Jenny was more touched than she should have been by this simple declaration. They clinked glasses and she took an appreciative taste of the surprisingly sharp, flinty wine, as different from the house wine as the house wine was from chocolate milk. If this was 'not bad', what did he usually drink?

'That's *delicious*,' she said, and set down her glass. 'You know, I keep forgetting that you've just been released. I must say that it looks like you got off lightly . . . considering.'

'You wouldn't think so if you saw my bruises.' He shook his head. 'I never knew there were so many shades of blue! But you're right, I got off very lightly. Actually, three or four days in the hospital would have been more than enough, but I stayed the week to please Bert . . . Bert Lathan, the friend I was staying with.' He shrugged. 'After turning his ultralight into a pile of sticks and rags, and worrying the hell out of him, the least I could do was follow his doctor's advice.'

It struck Jenny that while Paul's care for his friend's welfare was highly commendable, his concern for himself—and for those who had had to

come after him when he got himself into trouble—
was pretty rudimentary. What he needed was a good
talking-to, or maybe a good swift kick. Just because
he was rich, and charming, and a celebrity didn't
entitle him——

There she went again, out on a wavery limb she
had no business being on. Maybe she wasn't being a
brilliant conversationalist with Paul, but she was
certainly having a trenchant dialogue with herself.
In any case, she reminded herself severely, how Paul
Conan Brant the Third lived his life was none of her
business. None at all.

When their meals came Jenny was happy to see
that the chef hadn't had an off-night—for the town's
reputation, she told herself, not because it mattered
to her what Paul thought. As for herself—well,
salisbury steak would never be the same.

'Bert Lathan . . .' she said after a few delicious
bites. 'The name sounds vaguely familiar but I can't
place it.'

'He owns a ranch near Vista.'

'Oh, I see.'

Answers to several questions about what Paul
Brant was doing anywhere near Cochise Bend
clicked into place. He hadn't been very near it at all.
Vista was a little town near the Arizona-New
Mexico border about thirty miles away, and much
more his style. It was the gateway to the Chiricahua
Mountains on the other side of the range, the eastern
side. Jenny's rescue work had taken her through
there a few times and she had seen for herself that its
reputation as a country-clubbish residential retreat

was well deserved. The scenery had drawn some well-off Easterners who had bought old ranches or fruit orchards to play at, or who had simply bought whole mountains or canyons and built huge, showy homes there.

She had heard that most of them were 'snow-birds'—people who migrated south in the winter, and north in the spring to return to their mansions or family seats or whatever they were. This she really didn't know for sure, never having moved in such exalted circles. She was lucky to have one roof over her head, much less two.

While they ate, Paul regaled her with story after hilarious story of his friend's early days on the ranch, which he had bought under the delusion that pests such as rattlesnakes, and coyotes and mountain lions were things of the past, long ago rounded up and put in zoos. And when those stories ran out Paul led the conversation knowledgeably through an amazing variety of subjects from art to wine-making, to geology, to animal psychology.

And what was more amazing, he made them all fascinating. Apart from the evening's sticky beginnings, in fact, and the surprisingly distressing awareness that she was on the receiving end of gratitude and not personal interest, it was turning into one of the pleasantest times she had had in years. She had expected him to be witty and amusing; she hadn't expected to have her intellect stimulated. And maybe more than her intellect.

'Well, how about throwing caution to the wind?' he said, looking over the dessert menu. 'How does

"Chef Walter's Bavarian Cheesecake" sound? And coffee?'

'If I can have it smothered in strawberries, you're on,' Jenny replied. 'And yes, coffee for sure.'

Especially coffee. She didn't have wine very often, and she felt as if she were floating ten feet above the table, bumping gently against the ceiling. Besides that, being the focus of his attention was becoming increasingly disconcerting. There was more than gratitude in those cool, probing green eyes now, and she was embarrassed to think what he might be reading in hers.

When the waitress came back with the coffee and desserts she also had a brandy for Paul and a Grand Marnier for her. Jenny hadn't even heard him order them. And she certainly hadn't asked for hers. 'I probably shouldn't,' she sighed, eyeing the dark, golden liqueur. 'I have to be at work early tomorrow.'

'Ah, tomorrow. You shouldn't ever worry about tomorrow. The world has to end some time, you know, and tonight's as likely as any other. There may not be a tomorrow, so it never pays to deprive yourself of anything pleasant today.' He grinned suddenly, a flashing, boyish smile. 'I'm thinking of calling that Brant's Law.'

Looking back later, Jenny could see that the night's disastrous ending was inevitable from that point on, although things didn't appear to start going wrong until they left the hotel and Paul pulled the leather case with his car keys out of his pocket.

'Paul?' Jenny murmured. 'You're not going to drive, are you?'

He raised an eyebrow. 'And why not?'

'Because with a Scotch, most of a bottle of wine, and two brandies, you're just not in a condition to get behind the wheel. You might think you're in control of things, but you're not.' A rare, carefree laughter burbled in her voice. 'Neither am I. I'm not sure I'm in a condition to walk.'

The glow of the street lamps lit the arrogant, tight-lipped smile he gave her. 'Jenny, I know how to hold my drink. Believe me,' he said more quietly, almost grimly, 'if I wasn't in control of myself you'd know it.'

As feathery-headed as she was, she knew enough to ignore that last sentence. 'That's what men always say, and it's just not true. With all you've had to drink, I'd hate to guess what your blood alcohol level is.' Why was she taking that biting tone with him? It was herself she was angry with, not Paul Brant, and berating him wasn't going to get rid of the ache she'd carried in the pit of her stomach for four years.

'Paul,' she said more softly, 'I know you probably think I'm being kind of a ... well, a ...'

'Pill?' he said helpfully. 'Drip? Prude? Prig? No, what in the world would make me think anything like that?'

Jenny's blue-grey eyes glittered. She didn't know herself if she were closer to tears or rage. 'Suit yourself,' she said tightly. 'I'm walking home.'

She spun on her heel and strode away, head high. But her ears strained to hear if there was a sound behind her. Was he coming after her? Did she want him to? Did she hope with all her heart he wouldn't? How could it be that she didn't know which she wanted? All she could hear were her own echoing footsteps and her hammering heart, about equally loud.

'Wait a minute.' He was at her side, his hand on her arm. She closed her eyes, and the relief that washed over her answered her question of a moment before. 'I'll get a cab,' he said grimly. He was admitting defeat, and it sounded like he wasn't used to it.

'No, thanks,' she said perversely. Or maybe not so perversely. She might be relieved, but she was also angry and confused. And something else; frightened—or something very close to frightened. 'It's only a ten-minute walk. It would take longer than that for a taxi to get here.'

Actually the walk was closer to twenty minutes, and almost all uphill, but the bursting tension was suddenly too much for her, and a long, dark, solitary walk home sounded like heaven. 'And honestly, there's no need for you to come with me. You're just out of the hospital and——'

Paul's face darkened with anger. 'Forget it. I'm not letting you walk home alone.'

Jenny tilted her chin defiantly. 'I'm pefectly capable of taking care of myself, thank you. goodnight.'

To her vast irritation he fell into step with her, one long stride for every two of hers. He muttered something she didn't catch. It didn't matter; she got the general message.

'This is nothing but male chauvinism on your part,' she countered through gritted teeth. 'I don't need assistance getting home.' She speeded up her walk, but he kept up with her with no visible effort.

'Let's just say I'm humouring myself.' He made an impatient gesture with his hand. 'I'd feel guilty if you were hassled on the way home by some poor guy who didn't know that those sexy, blue-grey eyes and long, lovely legs are actually appendages on a very wet blanket.'

The blood, which had begun to rise at the offhanded compliment she had thought he'd been delivering, drained abruptly from her face at his final words. Continuing to stalk blindly forward, Jenny blinked back hot, unexpected tears.

Wet blanket! How could two simple words hurt so much? How could they bring it all back as if it had happened yesterday? 'Come on, Jim,' she'd laughed, 'don't be such a wet blanket!' And finally he had laughed too, and given in, and . . . Had it really been four years since he had died? Four lightning-swift years. Four years that seemed a lifetime.

A sudden step into nothingness jolted her out of the past. She had unknowingly stepped off the high kerb and would certainly have fallen but for Paul's quick reflexes.

'Would you mind not twisting an ankle?' he said brusquely. 'It's bad enough hiking uphill on a full stomach. I'd hate to have to carry you.'

Angrily, she wrenched her arm out of his grasp. 'I wouldn't let you carry me across a mud puddle,' she said, flashing him a look that should have shrivelled him on the spot.

It didn't. He laughed humourlessly. 'Wrong century. Men stopped doing that a long time ago. Even us chauvinists.' His brows arched mockingly. 'You know, I can't help wondering how you ever got involved in search-and-rescue work. I'd have thought doing needlework or baking cookies at an old people's home would have been all the excitement you could handle.'

That didn't even deserve an answer, and Jenny turned abruptly up a paved walk that led to a darkened house. It wasn't hers, but Paul had no way of knowing that and if he didn't go away and leave her this instant she was going to explode.

'Of course,' he continued sweetly, turning with her, 'they found a sufficiently daring job for you—holding the poor victim's hand and murmuring sweet words of encouragement . . . assuming, that is, that he's in a nice safe place, and not lying on a ledge somewhere.'

'For your information, Mr Brant——' she began hotly, but what was the point? Why bother to tell him that 'murmuring sweet words of encouragement' was a rotating assignment, and it just happened to be her turn when they found him? Besides, it wasn't something silly and old-womanish, the way he made it sound. It was vital; she had seen it pull more than one shocked, half-dead wilderness victim back from over the brink.

He waited for her to continue, his eyebrows lifted condescendingly. When she didn't, he went on, the edge to his voice razor-sharp. 'With your nerve, or should I say the lack thereof, the team would have a hard time finding anything else you could handle—now that people don't have to roll bandages any more.'

Through her anger, she was increasingly puzzled. Why was he being so bitterly sardonic, so ... ungentlemanly? He seemed to be goading her, stabbing at her with the sharp blade of his own anger. But what did he have to be so angry about? No, she didn't want to know; she didn't want to have anything to do with him. In his own arrogant, patronising way he was so very much like the reckless hothead she had once been, and she despised his rash, devil-may-care approach to life as much as she had once despised her own.

'That's very perceptive of you,' she replied with an icy smile. 'And now that you've pegged me so neatly, and gotten me safely to my doorstep, you can say good riddance, go your merry way, and forget all about me.' He'd better; what was she going to do if whoever lived there opened the door?

He gave her a stony, tight-lipped smile. 'That's just what I'm going to do my damnedest to do.'

It seemed like a self-delivered cue for him to spin on his heel and stomp back down the pavement, so that Jenny was caught completely by surprise when he pulled her roughly towards him instead. She was too stunned to resist the crushing impact of his mouth on hers, the ruthless parting of her lips, the frightening, thrilling pressure of his long, hard body arched against hers.

She had been aware all evening—far too aware—of the tingling, disturbing effect of his sexual power on her, but it hadn't prepared her for anything like this. Even if his arms hadn't pinioned her so that she could scarcely breathe, let alone struggle, she couldn't have—wouldn't have—pulled away, wouldn't have protested, wouldn't have done anything but exactly what she did do ... stand there with her head swimming and the dark world reeling around her; stand there with her face turned submissively up to his, dissolving in his arms as he seemed to drink from her very soul.

Her breathing was in a bad way when he finally pulled his head back, and his wasn't much better. For a fraction of a second they stood transfixed—looking more deeply into each other's eyes than she had known was possible. Then, as if a curtain had dropped, his face darkened and he was gone, leaving her staring after him, wide-eyed but unseeing.

As clearly as if he'd told her, Jenny knew, as well as she knew anything at that moment, that he had spent his week in the hospital thinking of her, just the way she'd dreamt it away thinking about him. And it was just as clear that Jenny Roberts in real life hadn't held a candle to the woman he had conjured up. But how could she? He had remembered her from a semi-conscious, pain-drugged haze, but she wasn't some dream-goddess who ruled a dark, star-studded domain high in the Chiricahuas, she was flesh and blood, and she had as many faults as anyone else. Maybe a few more. Slowly she shook her head. Who would have thought ...

How long would it take him to forget her? she wondered wryly. Even without trying his 'damnedest,' she bet it would be all of two or three days. A more important question was—how long was it going to take her to forget him?

CHAPTER FOUR

SITTING glumly at her kitchen table, Jenny eyed with distaste the scrambled eggs and sausage she had forced herself to prepare for breakfast. What with dinner's over-indulgence, the tumultuous scene afterwards, and a predictably restless night, she had awakened very much under the weather. But she had long ago taught herself the value of a hearty breakfast. Or rather she'd learned it in her first search-and-rescue training sessions. If she expected to be ready to head off into the wilderness at a moment's notice for two or three days—once it had been for six, most of it in a freezing December storm—she had to keep her body well-stoked with fuel.

Fuel. Smiling wryly at herself she picked at the food. After the way she had melted in Paul's arms last night it was pretty clear that pork sausage wasn't all her body craved.

How alive she had felt when he'd held her! And if red blood was flowing in her veins again, Paul Brant had done her a great service; he had made her remember what it felt like to be a woman, and no man had been able to do that in four years.

She was enormously grateful to him, even if she heartily hoped that she never saw him again. Paul Brant wasn't meant for her, anyway. He was like some free, soaring eagle that had fallen to earth, had a

47

brief, unlikely dalliance with a surprised hummingbird that had momentarily caught his fancy, and was
undoubtedly back where he belonged in the stratosphere by now—if he hadn't broken his neck driving
to Vista last night.

Reflectively she munched on a piece of toast.
Maybe Cochise County didn't run to eagles, but there
were plenty of hawks around. If she just let herself
become a little more receptive to their attentions,
someone was sure to attract her as much as Paul had.
Definitely. No question about it. Sure. She sighed and
pushed her plate away. She just wasn't hungry this
morning.

The sound of her beeper going off drove everything
from her mind, as it always did. Dashing to the
portable short-wave radio on the kitchen counter, she
was hit by a stomach-churning wave of anxiety. Paul
had had quite a few drinks last night. Maybe he *had*
run his car off the narrow road to Vista, and they had
just discovered his car at the bottom of a ravine. She
flipped on the switch, her fingers trembling.

Sheriff Langendorf's crisp, nasal voice pierced the
usual static. 'Attention Cochise Search-and-Rescue
Team. We have a report of a fall victim on a ledge in
Kiowa Canyon . . .'

Jenny sighed with relief. It couldn't be Paul!
Forcing her mind back to the radio, she made a
mental note to stop worrying about a man like Paul
Brant. If he couldn't be troubled to worry about
himself, she wasn't going to do it for him.

'. . . Report directly to the canyon pull-out half a

mile west of the old El Tigre Mine turn-off on BM 5582. Over.'

Kiowa Canyon. That was steep, dangerous country, as bad as where Paul's ultralight had gone down. She called in her response, notified the bank, hastily got into uniform shirt, jeans, jacket, and boots, and ran outside to start her car. The rest of her equipment was already in the boot.

At the pull-out only two automobiles were parked beside the Sheriff's patrol car. Jenny recognised the jeep as Jake Stevens', who usually acted as operations leader. That was good. A lean, ageless man who seemed carved out of wood, Jake's natural good sense always provided a calming effect, no matter how treacherous the rescue. The orange Ford Fiesta with the California licence plates obviously belonged to the victim.

Getting out of her car, Jenny could see that Jake hadn't been there long. A sheriff's deputy was explaining things, and a dishevelled, frantic woman in rock-climbing clothes was trying to answer questions but having a hard time getting hold of herself.

At a motion from Jake, Jenny joined him at the cliff's edge, leaving the deputy to try to settle the near-hysterical woman down. Dropping to their stomachs and inching forward along the overhang they got a good look down the vertical wall of the canyon. They could barely see the figure on the ledge far below, but they could see it well enough to tell it wasn't moving.

'It doesn't look good,' Jake said as they scrambled to their feet. 'And Hank's in Vegas——'

'Oh, no!' Jenny groaned.

Hank Thomson, one of the town's two car mechanics, was the rescue team's most experienced rock-climber. Six feet, three inches tall and two hundred and forty pounds of solid muscle—including forty pounds of it between the ears, one local wag had said—Hank could be counted on to wager on any object that moved . . . and most things that didn't. Fortunately for the team, if not for Hank, his luck was consistently bad, so that his jaunts to Las Vegas never lasted more than a day or two. But his timing couldn't have been worse in this case.

'Oh, yes. And even if the rest of them make it today, there's no way we're going to be able to get that guy off that ledge until we get some reinforcements from the Tucson team. They're on their way, but we better get down to him in the meantime, and see if he's— well, see what we can do for him.'

They didn't speak for a few moments, while Jake hammered pitons into the ground near the edge, and Jenny efficiently looped a long coil of rope around them and tied the ends. 'We'll use that new Canadian technique for solo descents,' Jake said. 'That way one of us can stay up here to co-ordinate things when the others arrive.' He looked up at her from his crouch. 'And that's you. I'm making you ops leader in my stead while I go down——'

'Let me go down,' Jenny interrupted. 'Please, Jake.' Avoiding his eyes, she checked the already-secure ropes. 'I've practised the new descent more than you have.'

It was true enough, but they both knew there was

more to it than that. There was a fractional pause, and then Jake made his decision. 'All right, Jenny, but there's more to search-and-rescue than dangling off a rope hundreds of feet above the ground. This is a team effort; that's what makes it work—and you've got to take your share of responsibility, the same as anyone else. You're gonna have to learn that.'

Relieved, but embarrassed at being scolded, Jenny bit her lip as she buckled the chin strap of her hard hat. In all her work with the team she had shied away from taking control or making decisions, and he was right to lecture her about it. Risking her own neck had always been easy enough—a means of atonement, a psychologist would probably say—but accepting responsibility for what others did, that was another thing. Still, she wasn't being fair. Nobody enjoyed it, but the others took their turns without complaint.

By the time she'd strapped on a first-aid pack and hooked an extra helmet and harness to her belt, she had come to a small but important decision.

'Jake, you're right. Look, I'll train and supervise our next volunteer—if you think I can handle it.'

'Handle it?' he returned with a lean-faced grin. 'Of course you can handle it! And it'll be a fine way to give yourself a taste of responsibility.'

It would be that, all right, Jenny thought wryly. Team members' lives were often in each other's hands, and a panicky, unknowledgeable, or otherwise ill-prepared trainee could mean a horrible disaster. She hoped she wouldn't regret this.

She was ready to go down. Jake had thrown one

line over the edge, and had checked over the other ropes she'd made fast to herself. She took a deep breath, gave him a thumbs-up sign, and swung over the edge in the way she'd been trained.

It was the first step of the rappel from an overhang that was nasty—that moment when you gave up the security of firm, lovely ground beneath your feet to hang, suspended by flimsy-looking ropes, your face to the sheer rock wall. Jenny never did it without remembering her father's advice.

'Never look down, kid,' her rock-climbing father had drawled the first time he'd coached her over an edge at the age of twelve. 'If your rope system's good, you're safe as houses, but seeing all that nothing below you is enough to make you lose your breakfast.'

With not much breakfast to lose and a high probability of missing lunch, Jenny didn't look down. For a heart-stopping moment she dangled free in the air, like a spider hanging on a strand, but once she swung herself gently against the rock-face and got her feet propped against it, she expelled her breath, pushed off, and let herself down the two hundred yards to the ledge in a series of long, easy, floating hops.

She grimaced at the grotesque angles at which the deadly-pale, unconscious man's legs were bent beneath him. Both broken, obviously. No blood, though; at least they weren't compound fractures. But it would be a long time before he walked again. Of course, he was lucky to be alive at all, she thought grimly—if he was. To her relief, when she laid two fingers against the side of his throat she felt a rapid, shallow pulse beat, and her touch made him turn his head slightly and murmur something incoherent. On the chance that something might get through, she began speaking to him in a soothing murmur while she got to work.

Digging in her heels for a more secure foothold, if any foothold could be called secure on this narrow, precarious lip of rock, she gently and quickly fixed the safety harness under the limp arms and strapped the helmet to his head. She didn't like the look of their situation at all. The ledge was riddled with cracks, ready to fracture off entirely and leave them dangling from their ropes against the vertical cliff-face.

She unclipped her short-wave radio. 'Rescue one here. This ledge isn't very stable, but for the moment we're both safe as—well, we're safe. Victim's unconscious. Simple fractures of both legs. No other injuries apparent.'

'Roger.' Jake's voice crackled in the dry air. 'I can see our rescue truck down by the Dry Lake cut-off, so we should be down to you with splints and stretcher in about ten minutes. Tucson team's on their way too, coming as fast as they can. Out.'

Ten minutes. And what then? It would be pretty much impossible to winch a stretcher case upwards with that overhang. They would have to lower him to the floor of the canyon and carry him from there. But it was going to be tricky. Maybe the best thing to do would be to rig a traverse across the narrow canyon— it could be anchored at that formation they called Dead Horse Point—then pull the stretcher to the other side, and lower it from there. With all those

rock outcroppings and ledges it would be a lot easier.
Still, she was glad it wasn't her decision.

That thought brought her up short. It hadn't been
much over five minutes ago that she'd promised
Jake—and herself—to take on more responsibility,
and here she was running from the very thought of it.
Darn Hank and his ridiculous gambling expeditions!
With his climbing skills, it would hardly be necessary
to make a decision at all. He would have been down
this wall and up the opposite one in twenty minutes,
with a rope system rigged a few minutes after that.
Without him, they had no climbers with the necessary
skills; they would have to wait until the more
experienced Tucson team arrived.

And she wasn't sure how long the pallid, deathly
still young man on the ledge could wait. She knew
about the broken legs; she didn't know what might
have happened to him inside.

That was the problem with a small team like theirs.
With only ten members, not all of whom could show
up for every mission, their role on difficult rescues like
this one was often to helplessly hold the fort until the
Tucson team got there. What they really needed was a
real climber, better even than Hank—somebody like
Paul Brant . . .

For the second time in a minute she had startled
herself. Paul Brant! What had made that infuriating,
arrogant——

The rope that dangled from the cliff-top to the
ledge twitched at the same moment that a sandy spray
of pebbles showered down from above. She jerked her
head up, shielding her eyes from the sun. Good! Part

of the Tucson team must have flown in.

One of them was rappelling down to join her with an effortless competence that made her envious. It must be Les Forrester, the surprisingly plump little man who had learned to climb in Yosemite. She shook her head with admiration. If she ever learned to move even half that well——

Squinting against the naked sunlight, she frowned. That wasn't Les—not with that athletic, mobile torso and those long, powerfully graceful legs. Well, whoever it was, she was more than happy to see him.

'Hi!' she shouted up as he got to within fifty feet of the ledge. 'I'm glad——'

It couldn't be! How could it be possible? With her eyes popping and her mouth agape with disbelief she must have looked like a hooked fish, but she couldn't do anything other than stare as a long, perfectly timed, final hop put the roped figure down on the ledge, feather-light, a scant five yards away from her.

The sudden stoppage of motion jarred her enough so she remembered to snap her mouth closed before Paul Brant turned his head to look in her direction. To her immense satisfaction he was as startled as she had been. Not, of course, that he would do anything as inelegant as gape. Hardly. No, he simply looked briefly incredulous—that is, his right eyebrow rose an eighth of an inch for about an eighth of a second—and then his jaw tightened into an even squarer line than usual.

'What—what are you doing here?' she stammered. 'How did you get here?'

'On a rope,' he practically growled. He glanced

quickly at the unconscious man, and then turned his back on her to hammer pitons into a crack in the rock-face with furious energy.

But what was he so angry about? Was it her fault that he had leapt to the disdainful conclusion that she was good for nothing but 'murmuring soothing words of encouragement in nice, safe places'? Her only sin was that she hadn't corrected him, and he could hardly be angry about that. Except, of course, that he very obviously was. Doubtless, he didn't eat crow very often, and he wasn't finding it palatable!

It didn't stop him from going about his work with cold, detached efficiency. When the pitons were secure, he held out his hand, barely looking at her. 'Radio,' he commanded.

Submissively, she gave him her radio. If it had been any other time or place, she would have hit him with it.

'Brant here,' he said crisply into it. 'Send down the stretcher and some leg splints. Looks like a broken right femur and left tibia; maybe the fibula too. Over and out.'

He handed the radio back to her and surveyed the terrain. 'It's not going to be easy,' he said, talking more to himself than to her. 'The cliff-face is too smooth, and there's too much overhang at the top.'

'I know,' Jenny said. 'I thought we might——'

'A traverse, that's what we need. It shouldn't be too hard to rig one up with the canyon this narrow.' His sharp eyes scanned the other side. 'The only question is, where do we anchor it over there . . .?'

'I thought a good place would be——'

'There,' he announced summarily, 'that point with all the pink granite.'

'Dead Horse Point,' she muttered through clenched jaws.

'Whatever. Here comes the stretcher. Once we get our man splinted and strapped into it, I'll go down to the floor and scale up to the point. We'll have him out in no time.'

He reached up for the aluminium stretcher and the first-aid supplies, looking over his shoulder at her. 'You know, I'd have thought that even you would have figured that out.'

Grr, she snarled mentally, *what I wouldn't give . . .* But she gritted her teeth and bore it, working at Paul's side on the splinting, through which the young man remained mercifully unconscious.

When Paul swung out again into the canyon, Jenny was staggered by his speed and expertise. It was one thing to know these badlands would be child's play to a man who had climbed the world's premier mountain, but it was another thing to see him in action. How could he have such skill—such hard-won skill—and not want to put it to regular, productive use?

Almost miraculously, the injured climber was on the floor of Kiowa Canyon by the time the Tucson team arrived. All that was left to do was to carry the stretcher up-canyon to where the walls widened enough to allow the Sheriff's helicopter to fly in and retrieve it. That was quickly accomplished, and the helicopter had swiftly clattered off towards Tucson General Hospital.

As always at the end of a successful mission, the air crackled with exuberance, and there was laughter and self-congratulation when the call came from the medic on the helicopter: the patient was doing fine, with no sign of head or internal injuries.

'Well, I can see you guys don't need us any more,' shouted the black-bearded driver of the Tucson truck as he turned the key in the ignition. 'Not with the Great Man himself on your team.'

'I just wish he was,' Jake called back with a frankly admiring glance at Paul. 'Tell you what, Mr Brant,' he added more quietly, 'any time you get tired of life in the fast lane, come see me. I think we just might find a place for you.'

Jenny wasn't looking in their direction, but a cold tingle at the nape of her neck told her Paul was looking at her. Unable to help herself, she glanced up from the rope she was coiling.

He was looking at her all right, with an all-but-unreadable expression in his eyes and in the tight-lipped set of his mouth. She didn't know how to interpret it, but something inside her did, because the tingle abruptly expanded, crawling all the way down to the small of her back and then up again across her scalp, so it was all she could do to repress a shiver.

For what seemed like minutes, but could only have been a moment or two, he held her gaze with the sheer, hypnotic power of those piercing green eyes. This, she thought confusedly, must be the way a field-mouse feels when it's mesmerised by a hungry snake. At last he released her. His eyes softened, the firm line of his mouth relaxed to something approaching a smile, and he turned to Jake.

'How about now?' he said calmly.

'How about what now?' Jake said.

'How about finding a place for me on the team now?'

Jenny's heart stopped for an instant, and then started again, double-time. Why was he leading Jake on? What sort of game was he playing with them? What was he *doing* here at all?

Jake looked as surprised as she was, although she doubted if his heart were racing. 'I just wish you were serious,' he said tentatively.

'I've never been more serious,' Paul countered. Drily, he added, 'Or don't I meet the qualifications?'

Jake was still sceptical. 'All but living locally,' he replied, equally drily.

'That's no problem. I've already committed myself to spending some time here.'

'Then, of course, there's a probationary and training period . . .'

And let's see you put that in your pipe and smoke it, Jenny thought, ready to throttle Paul for putting on the sincere and good-natured Jake this way. Jake gave more of himself in a month, and did more good than the Paul Brants of this world did in their whole lives.

Paul just shrugged and gestured at the communications and medical gear the team was packing away.

'I'm not surprised. I can see there's more to rescue work than rock-climbing.'

You bet there is, mister, Jenny said silently. There's getting out of a warm bed to clamber through freezing mud at three o'clock in the morning, and——

'So when do I start?' Paul said.

If Jenny wasn't convinced, Jake finally was. His face crinkled into a broad smile. 'The sooner the better. There are a lot of details for Jenny to teach you.'

You better believe it, Jenny nodded to herself in grim agreement. More details than you'd—— *What* had Jake said? Alarmed, she looked up quickly from the ropes.

'Me?' she practically squeaked.

'Sure,' Jake said, surprised. 'You offered just this morning to take on the next trainee, remember?'

Stifling a groan of dismay, Jenny glanced anxiously at Paul, fighting down a sudden tide of panic at the amusement flickering in his cool, green eyes. The thought of being thrown into contact with him, even for the few days it would take him to tire of this absurd little amusement he had dreamed up, sent chills travelling along her spine again. This had more bright red danger signs stamped on it than a case of dynamite.

All the same, she could hardly go back on her word to Jake.

'Y-Yes,' she stammered. 'Of course I remember.'

'Good, that's settled.' Jake beamed avuncularly at both of them and went off to help with the clear-up.

Her blue-grey eyes storming, Jenny lowered her voice so only Paul could hear her.

'How dare you be so insensitive? What are you doing, having your lordly fun at the expense of the gullible clodhoppers? Jake Stevens is the finest, most self-sacrificing man I've ever met, worth a dozen of you! His hardware store is closed right now, because some stranger he'd never heard of had a fall. And for you to lead him on . . . as if you'd really give your time . . . Oh, what's the use?'

Paul had listened to her speech with his hands resting informally on his narrow hips, and no reaction other than a maddeningly condescending smile on his superior face.

'Are you out of words or out of breath?' he asked, still grinning.

'Just out of polite words,' she snapped, near to trembling with suppressed anger.

'Well, before you think up any impolite ones, can I get in a word? Make that three words: I . . . am . . . serious. I want to join the team, Jenny.'

'But—but that's ridiculous,' she sputtered. 'I've read about you, you know. You couldn't stick to one interest, or one job, or . . . or one woman longer than a week if your life depended on it!' She flung the words at him.

'Well,' he said softly, 'you shouldn't believe everything you read in the papers.' One of his eyebrows lifted, and his eyes, fixed on her own, turned speculative in a way that sapped the strength distressingly from her knees.

'As for my love life,' he went on slowly, 'was that a personal challenge you were offering? Because if it is . . .' Now his eyes roved openly over her, sliding down, and then up, leaving in their path a thrilling, quivering rush that she wasn't ready to admit, even to herself. '. . . if it is, I might take you up on it. You just might turn out to be amusing company. Out of bed as well as in it, I mean—which is more than I can say for most women.'

'This conversation is getting ridiculous!' she cried, blushing beet-red. 'What makes you think . . .? Why are we . . .? How can you . . .?' She ground to a halt like a phonograph with a snapped needle, as furious at herself as she was at him. 'You know I didn't mean any such thing! I have absolutely no interest in your love life. I couldn't care about it less. I was just using an example.'

'Uh-huh,' he said with a taunting smile that unnerved her even more. 'And you always blush when you use examples.'

Jenny drew herself up as tall as she could. 'This,' she declared glacially, 'is getting us nowhere. I don't believe for a minute you're sincere about joining the team, but I'll do what Jake expects me to do. Tomorrow's Saturday, so we'll start then. Eight sharp, at the Sheriff's car-pool garage. Now, if you'll excuse me, I have to finish helping Jake pack the gear, and then I have to go to work.'

She turned sharply on her heel, then swung around to face him again. 'That's eight o'clock in the *morning*, Mr Brant. If you think you can get out of bed that early!'

He grinned back at her. 'No problem. Nothing to keep me there. At the moment.'

She retreated with her mind a muddle of conflicting thoughts and emotions, some murderous, some confused, and some startlingly unladylike indeed.

None of which, she was uncomfortably sure, would have surprised Paul Brant in the least.

CHAPTER FIVE

THE NEXT day dawned clear, so that by eight the sun was already starting to burn off the night-time desert chill. It was perfect for what Jenny had in mind if Paul actually showed up.

When she drove into the parking space in front of the Sheriff's garage she wasn't surpised to see no sign of a white Porsche. But the long, noisy breath she expelled startled her. She had had no idea that she'd been holding her breath. Was it a sigh of relief or of disappointment? Before she could honestly answer, the sleek, snow-white automobile turned the corner behind her, appearing in her rear-view mirror as it slowed to a smooth halt.

Bracing herself, her heart thumping, she pulled on the handbrake and climbed out.

'I'm glad you're on time,' she said, with as cool a tone as she could muster. 'We've lots of things to do.'

Paul smiled lazily. 'Good thing I wore jeans,' he said, taking in her clothes. 'It looks like we're in for some grubby work.'

'*You're* in for some grubby work,' Jenny rejoined drily. 'I'm the supervisor, remember?'

'Yes, *ma'am!*' he grinned, snapping his fingers to his temple in a crisp salute.

Laugh away, my bucko, she thought as they walked into the garage by a side entrance. You'll be doing some useful work this morning, for once in your overprivileged life.

Even if there weren't a messy job ahead, she would still have dressed in her oldest, most patched cords, a T-shirt, and tennis shoes that were more holes than anything else. Pigtails over her ears and a total absence of make-up completed what seemed to her a convincing imitation of a scroungy, puppyish teen-ager. It was the best strategy she could think of to offset any ideas Paul might have about her interest in him. And it was hardly likely, she thought wryly, to add fuel to whatever interest he thought he had in her.

'What do we start with, chief?' he asked cheerfully. 'I'm pretty up-to-date in first aid, but I suppose I could use some rescue equipment familiarisation. There are also some radio operation details that I could stand——'

'We start with washing the rescue truck.'

'Washing the ... the ...'

'Truck,' she supplied helpfully. She had to bite her lip to keep from bursting into laughter at his expression. 'You'll find buckets and detergent over by the sink.'

Without waiting for his reply, she hopped into the big van and drove it out into the paved space, pleased with the way she'd handled things so far, but tremblingly conscious of standing at the edge of a dangerous precipice. *Without a rope system!*

She parked the truck in a sunny spot near the hose, and was giving it a preliminary spray to take off yesterday's dust when Paul emerged grimly from the garage, armed with buckets and sponges.

'Is this standard trainee practice?' he demanded

with a dark look. 'Or Jenny Roberts' very own funny idea?'

Jenny turned off the tap, took one of the buckets from him, and set it near the rear wheel. 'I hate to disillusion you so early, but there are a lot of dull chores involved in rescue work. In fact, there are a lot of dull missions. Sorry about that.'

'Sure, you're sorry,' he shot back, and for a moment Jenny thought he was going to call it quits and stride back to his car. Instead he dropped a sponge into the soapy, hot water and got energetically to work. His mouth was set in a straight line, but there was amusement in his voice when he spoke. 'You still think I'm not on the level, don't you?'

'Yes, I do, but for as long as you want to keep enjoying your little game or whatever it is, I can at least get some useful work out of you. There are medical supplies to be restocked, ropes to be inspected and recoiled . . .'

He was kneeling down, not paying much attention to her, scrubbing at the road grease behind the tyres, and she took advantage of the opportunity to take in the way the firm muscles of his shoulders were thrown into relief against his green Oxford shirt, and his long, well formed thighs strained against his corduroy jeans. An undeniably attractive man, Paul Brant; darned attractive. From a physical point of view, anyway. In every other way, totally, utterly infuriating.

'By the way,' she said, prudently turning her eyes back to the truck, 'just how did you get involved yesterday?'

'Sheer rotten luck, I'm starting to think,' he

muttered. 'I was having breakfast when one of your team members—Ted, I think his name is—recognised me.'

'Ted Beckman?' she exclaimed, surprised. 'The gardener at the Copper King Hotel?'

'That's him. He was on his way out, and he said your group was missing its best climber, and could I lend a hand?'

'You mean you spent Thursday night at the hotel here in Cochise Bend, and I——' Jenny stopped abruptly. It wouldn't do at all to let him see how anxious she'd been for him.

At the tone in her voice he glanced up from his work at her, his head tilted. His hair fell boyishly over his forehead, as it had the night she'd first seen him, and again she glanced quickly away, troubled at the feelings he could rouse in her without even trying. Without caring, either.

'Don't flatter yourself,' he said, continuing to misread her expressions with regularity. 'I checked in that afternoon, before I talked to you at the bank,' he drawled, 'so you can rest assured you didn't have anything to do with it.' He sat back on his heels, a half-sheepish smile on his face. 'Just as I don't flatter myself that it was my little lecture on wet-blanketness that motivated you to deeds of daring on narrow ledges. You don't learn that kind of rock-climbing overnight.'

He rested a forearm on each thigh, and looked quizzically at her with one eyebrow lifted, in that way he had. 'Now why the hell did you let me go on like that?'

Jenny shrugged, dipped a sponge into her bucket,

and began to go over the side of the van with soapy water.

'I suppose,' she said after a moment, 'it was because in some ways it's true. I *am* a wet blanket.' With the back of her hand she brushed a tendril of ash-brown hair from her eyes. 'I don't like to see people taking risks with their lives—except for worthwhile objectives.'

'Like saving other people's lives?'

'Yes.'

'You might have something there,' he mused. Straightening, he stretched his long body and started to soap down a front fender. 'I have to admit it was really something to see that woman's face when the medic radioed back that her friend was going to be all right.'

'Is that why you suddenly decided to join?'

'No,' he said, 'and yes.' Maddeningly, he wouldn't offer any further explanation, but his green eyes compelled hers to meet them. 'And you might as well get it into that pretty, pigtailed head right now that I'm dead serious about it.'

'You'll never last the course,' Jenny returned briskly, hiding her dismay at the steely certainty in his voice.

Paul Brant stirred her senses far too acutely, and the training would throw them together for days at a time. For her, at least, she knew that a physical attraction—which was putting it mildly, in this case—could be the first long step towards love, and if she weren't careful she would find herself falling head over heels for him.

And that, muzzy as her thoughts might be these

days, she knew she didn't want. The idea of an unrequited love, just as she finally seemed to be getting over a dead one, seemed too awful to be borne.

'So I might as well quit now?' he said, the muscles in his jaw tensing. 'Is that what you'd like?'

'It would certainly save us all a lot of trouble.'

His eyes suddenly narrowed with a sardonic, knowing gleam. 'Do you want me to tell you what's bothering you? If you ask me it's——'

'I didn't ask you, and I'm not the least little bit interested in——'

'——pretty damned obvious. You're afraid you're falling for me, aren't you? You're worried about us being thrown together.'

She gasped. Was she transparent, after all? 'Really, this is . . . Of all the silly, egotistical——'

'Do you think I didn't notice what happened when I kissed you the other night?' He grinned, remembering. 'You practically melted into a puddle at my feet.'

'*Melted!*' she echoed with an unconvincing attempt at an incredulous laugh. 'Into a . . . a . . .'

'Puddle,' he supplied with a grin. 'At my feet. I've hit on it, haven't I?'

She took a deep breath and got a tenuous grip on herself. 'These fantasies of yours are very entertaining, but the job at the moment is washing the truck. So let's get on with it.' She laid on the sponge with renewed vigour.

Paul wasn't having any of it. He tossed his sponge into a bucket and leaned against the truck, arms folded, and one leg crossed casually over the other. He was still grinning. 'That's why you got yourself camouflaged as Raggedy Ann, or Huckleberry Finn, or whatever you're supposed to be.' The smile faded. 'Isn't it?'

'The answer to that is no. Definitely, absolutely, positively——'

'Uh-huh,' he said, his smile returning. That's what I thought.'

Nettled, Jenny flung her sponge into the bucket and tilted her chin aggressively up. 'For a man who doesn't flatter himself, it certainly seems to me that you're taking an awful lot for granted. Let me assure you,' she prevaricated, 'I could spend days—*weeks*—in your presence without so much as a flutter of the pulse. Except with exasperation, of course!'

That, she thought, was pretty good, but Paul only threw back his head and laughed. 'You know,' he said drily, 'I'm inclined to take a remark like that as a personal challenge.'

She opened her mouth to protest, but he cut her off.

'The future's getting more interesting by the minute,' he said, suddenly thoughtful. 'It looks as if we both have something to prove.'

With that, he bent agilely to pick up his bucket, broke into a cheerful whistle, and headed around to the truck's front.

Jenny contemplated emptying her own bucket at his retreating back, but decided it would only make things worse. She hadn't won a skirmish yet this morning, and there was no sense in starting another. She was going to have to be a lot more clever than she'd been so far.

It was noon by the time they finished restocking the supplies, and Jenny called it quits for the day. Except for comments on first-aid equipment, ropes, and two handbooks she'd given him to read, they hadn't said a word to each other in three hours.

'Busy tonight?' Paul asked offhandedly, as they walked towards their cars.

Could he really be serious? She knew the best thing she could say would be a simple, unadorned 'yes', but she couldn't help responding to the lilting taunt in his voice.

'Why, so you can test your little theory out?'

He grinned. 'The thought occurred to me, but actually, no. I mentioned you to Bert and Peg Lathan last night, and they'd like to meet you. They told me to bring you out to the ranch for dinner if you're free on such short notice.'

He opened her door, then leaned both elbows on it. 'Of course, if you're frightened of being with me,' he said, his eyes glinting devilishly, 'you won't want to come. Would you like a little time to think up an excuse? I'm not in a hurry.'

'Sorry to disappoint you,' she said, feeling oddly like an animal at bay, 'but I'm not the least frightened of being with you, and I wouldn't dream of inventing an excuse. As it happens, I love ranches, and I'd like to visit the Lathans.'

'Fine,' Paul said neutrally. 'I'll pick you up at five.'

Not on his life, he wouldn't! She was not about to subject herself to an intimate round-trip drive of sixty miles with him. Washing a truck with him was tough enough.

'No need to pick me up,' she said smoothly. 'I have some things to take care of out that way this afternoon. What time shall I be there?'

* * *

Dressing down hadn't done her any good, so Jenny decided that she might as well look her best. If nothing else, it would give her some self-assurance, and she knew she would need all of that that she could get.

She started with a hot shower, a shampoo, and a sorely needed manicure. Then she blow-dried her thick hair—her best feature, she thought—into long, loose waves that lay densely on her shoulders. Make-up was low-key, except for a luscious peach lip-gloss that she applied without letting herself think about why she'd picked it. It wasn't to make an impression on the Lathans, that much she was sure of.

Choosing her clothes was easy. She had only one sophisticated outfit—a turquoise jumpsuit.

With its collared V-neck and figure-hugging shape, the brushed corduroy suit was far more elegant than a jumpsuit had any right to be. It was dressy without being formal; in fact, it was just right for the Southwest's casual, if trendy, approach to social engagements. Fortunately, a simple Zuni Indian pendant of silver and pale green turquoise, and matching ear-rings, were all the jewellery needed to set it off.

She debated on whether to wear high heels or flats, and decided to go with the high. Three inches added to her barefoot five foot and nine inches, and she'd be almost eye to eye with Paul Brant. Just let him try to intimidate her tonight!

The Lathans' Lyre Creek Ranch was even more beautiful than Jenny had anticipated and, once she had parked the old Buick on the sandy, circular drive, she sat back in the seat and took it all in for a minute. Nestled in the rolling eastern foothills of the

Chiricahuas, the ranch buildings sprawled in a tree-dotted canyon of oaks, pines, and junipers. The main house was a great, rambling white-painted place of long, sloping roofs and wide verandas—everybody's idea of what a ranch house ought to be. The big barn also lived up to expectations, sufficiently decrepit to be romantic, but obviously sturdy enough to do its job. Behind it were two split-rail corrals in which several horses placidly munched their hay, and further off a few neatly maintained little cottages.

Except for the gigantic, free-form swimming pool near the cottages, she might have been looking at a scene from a hundred years ago. To finish the bucolic picture, the aptly named Lyre Creek itself purled and tinkled nearby, a real treasure in this arid country where 'creeks' and 'rivers' usually had water in them for only two or three weeks of the year, during the winter storms.

It was sheer heaven! When Jenny was a child, she had dreamed of living in a place like this. She still did, only now she was old enough to know it was nothing but a dream. Ah, well, it was lovely to be there, even for an evening, and she was grateful to Paul for that much, anyway. She took a deep breath of the juniper-laden air and headed for the front door.

Bert Lathan was a distinct surprise. She knew that he was an old friend of Paul's, that he flew ultralights for fun—or had, until Paul had smashed his Eagle VI—and that he had moved here from the East only a few years ago. As a result, without even realising it she had been expecting someone like Paul himself: smooth, sophisticated and cosmopolitan. And wickedly attractive!

But the scholarly, fragile-looking man who opened the door was the exact opposite of Paul. With his horn-rimmed glasses, tightly curled red hair and pale complexion, he looked as if he'd spent his whole life behind a book in a university research library.

And, apparently, she wasn't what he'd had in mind, either.

'No!' he said, framed in the doorway, a gleam of humour lighting his gentle blue eyes. '*You're* Jenny Roberts? Oh, my!'

She smiled, liking him on sight. 'I gather I'm not quite what was expected.'

He smiled too. '"Not quite" is an understatement. I believe Paul said something about a pair of pigtails and a Huckleberry Finn wardrobe.' His smile tipped up humorously on one side. 'But he did admit that you weren't too terribly bad-looking when seen in the right light.'

Laughing, Jenny couldn't help returning the open friendliness of the man. 'Think he'll be disappointed that I didn't live up to his expectations? Or should I say *down*?'

'Well, let's just say I'll enjoy being there when he sees you. Come into the kitchen, Jenny. Paul's in there helping Peg—that's my wife.'

Both Jenny and Bert were amply rewarded by the look on Paul's face at the sight of her.

'Er ... um ... hello,' he stammered, very nearly dropping the platter in his hand. Jenny bit back a giggle. It was delicious to see him at a loss for words for once. 'Ah ... Peg, this is, er, Jenny.'

Peg Lathan was a couple of inches taller than her husband; a plump, lively, talkative woman with a

gravelly voice and laughter crinkles around her eyes.
She exuded the same ready hospitality that Bert did,
and within a few minutes Jenny was wondering
where well-to-do Easterners got their reputation for
snobbishness. She could call Paul Brant a lot of things
(she already had, in fact), but stuffy wasn't one of
them, and his friends seemed cut from the same
mould.

'Take a stool and let's you and I watch them work,
Jenny,' Bert suggested. 'We're all drinking Chablis,
but I have a Green Hungarian keeping cold, if you'd
like to match that marvellous outfit.' He looked
sideways at Paul, and Jenny managed to read with
pleasure the wry message in his glance: *Huckleberry
Finn*?

'Chablis will be fine, thanks.' Things were going
well so far, but she wasn't taking any chances; she
didn't know whether a Green Hungarian was a wine,
a liqueur, or a seasick Eastern European.

Peg was efficiently engaged with four beautifully
fresh whole trout, all rose and silver. Watching her
stuff each fish with mixed herbs, cloak it in fresh dill
sprigs, and then pass it to Paul for tying up with
string, Jenny could see that gourmet cooking was an
everyday affair in the Lathans' kitchen. And if Peg's
expertise hadn't made that clear, the kitchen itself
would have. It was an absolute dream, just about as
roomy as Jenny's entire apartment, and filled with
gleaming, modern equipment, including a big barbe-
cue grill, under a vent, set into a blue and yellow
Spanish-tiled counter. A pyramid-shaped pile of
charcoal briquettes was heaped in the centre, waiting
to be lit.

'I'd love to help,' Jenny said. 'May I?'

'You'd better believe it,' Peg smiled. 'We can use it. Bert, get that Mother Hubbard apron out of the bottom drawer for Jenny so she doesn't get anything on that terrific suit . . . And keep your paws out of those pine nuts.'

'Are you speaking to me?' Bert protested angelically. 'Pine nuts, did you say?'

'Yes, pine nuts. I think we'd better let Jenny make the spinach and nut salad right now. That is, if we want to have any nuts in it.'

'Very well,' said Bert haughtily, 'since you don't appear to trust me.'

'Not an inch. You can skewer the scallops. I think raw scallops would be safe even from *you*.' She turned to Jenny. 'It's disgusting. He eats anything he wants and never gains an ounce, while I . . .' She shook her head ruefully. 'If you ask me, life is very unfair.' She rinsed her hands after finishing with the last fish. 'If he reaches for a nut, you whack him with that spoon. Hard. Where it hurts.'

Bert's eyes rolled up. 'My God, the woman's an absolute tyrant. Why do I put up with it? My next wife's going to be as docile as a lamb. And I think I'll try a blonde. Yes, I'll definitely try a blonde.'

'Jenny, will you hit him with the spoon, anyway? On general principles?'

Jenny smiled. It was impossible not to see how much they liked each other. And something told her very clearly that, as physically unmatched as they seemed to be, there was no problem whatever on that score. She couldn't help being just a little envious. So much warmth, so much love . . . Were they there for her too, in her future?

She had kept her emotions in cold storage for so long that it frightened her to have them begin to break free the way they had in the last few weeks. But she wasn't going to coop them up again. Not ever. She wanted more from life than she had been admitting to herself. She wanted what Bert and Peg had, and surely there was somebody out there for her. Somewhere.

Involuntarily, her eyes strayed to Paul, but when he met them head-on with his own arrogant green gaze and the ghost of a smile, she dropped them quickly back to the spinach leaves she was destemming. She might not be able to control her nervous system when he was around, but she could control her life, and Paul Brant, as devilishly attractive as he was, wasn't a very good bet for a long-term relationship.

As the dinner preparations moved along, she discovered that Paul was as comfortable in the kitchen as the Lathans were. While Peg prepared a side dish of wild rice and mushrooms, and Bert worked on the skewers, he made a dill sauce for the seafood, using a cleaver to chop the herbs with the flair and speed of a chef. She wasn't surprised. She suspected that he was good at anything he wanted to try. What an absolutely infuriating man!

By the time they all sat down to charcoal-grilled scallops and trout, there had been so much good talk and by-play that she felt as comfortable with the Lathans as if they'd been old friends. That didn't go for Paul, of course. How did you get comfortable around a man who made your knees watery and set every nerve-ending in your spine tingling simply by reaching around you for a long-handled wooden spoon?

Afterwards, when they were all lounging like overstuffed walruses in front of the ceiling-high fieldstone fireplace in the living-room, the talk turned to occupations. Bert was an architect, Jenny learned to her surpise, for she had assumed that, despite his bookish appearance, he led the same life of adventure and pleasure Paul did. And Peg turned out to be an illustrator of scientific textbooks.

'One of the best,' Paul interjected. 'Peg, you'll have to show Jenny those botanical sketches you're working on for Prentice-Hall.'

'I'd love to see them,' Jenny said honestly.

'I'll bring them out after dessert and coffee,' Bert said, lost somewhere in the lumpy furrows of a floppy bean bag chair. 'I suppose they have a certain amusement value.'

'It's so terrific to have a supportive spouse,' Peg laughed. 'Thank *you*, anyway, Mr Brant.' she re-arranged her sofa cushion and settled back with a contented sigh. 'Anyway, illustrating has turned out to be great work for me because I can do it
his assignments. Not that that's any great privilege, mind you, but it gives me a chance to get out and see the world.'

Bert ignored the last sentence. 'I design mostly civic architecture,' he explained, 'and that usually takes some on-site inspection, so I'm in the field for a week or two at a time.'

'What about you, Jenny?' Peg asked.

'I work in a bank,' Jenny confessed, wishing she

could have said something a lot more impressive. 'I'm a teller. I'm afraid it gets a bit dull at times.'

'I imagine you have more than enough excitement,' Peg replied, sliding a wry glance in Paul's direction, 'when you're busy plucking careless pilots out of the Chiricahuas.'

'I get the distinct impression,' Paul drawled ruefully, turning from the fireplace, where he'd been rearranging the logs with a poker, 'that Peg's never going to let me live that down.'

With difficulty, Bert pushed himself into a more or less upright sitting position in the soft chair, and peered at Paul over his bony knees.

'Don't let her fool you. She couldn't be more delighted about your total destruction of my poor ultralight—although she claims she regrets the bruises you suffered in doing it.'

Peg grinned. 'You're not telling Paul anything he doesn't already know. The last thing I need is to have my husband floating around in the stratosphere, strapped into something made of toothpicks and tissue paper.'

'Toothpicks and tissue paper,' Bert muttered, dropping back into the chair with a mournful sigh. 'Astonishing, the ignorance I have to put up with.'

'And don't think you're getting another one, pal. I chewed my fingernails more than enough while you were up in the last one.'

Bert stroked his chin, considering. 'A blonde,' he said solemnly. 'Yes, definitely a blonde next time.'

'I think I'm going to leave the pips in his cherries jubilee,' Peg said, rising from the sofa. 'Who wants coffee with dessert?'

Turning down all offers of help, she invited Jenny to join her in the kitchen.

'At least let me make the coffee,' Jenny said, watching Peg select a jar of black cherries from the pantry.

'Sure, if you want. You'll find everything you need in the cupboard next to the microwave.'

'Have you known Paul long?' Jenny asked, opening the cupboard door.

'Practically for ever. Bert and Paul date back to prep school days, and I met them both in college. We see him every year or so, but this is the first time we've gotten him out to the ranch. I can hardly believe he's offered to oversee things while we're in Ecuador.'

'You're going to Ecuador?'

'Oh, didn't I mention it? Yes, we're leaving at the end of next week for two months. Bert's going to be working on a fantastic project—a whole model city centre. I get excited every time I think about it. I just hope Paul doesn't change his mind about looking out for the ranch.'

'Is he the sort of person who'd do that?'

'No, not at all,' Peg said quickly, noting Jenny's frown. 'It's just that he's not the kind of person to stay that long in any one place. Actually, we wouldn't have dreamed of asking him, but they got to talking about it during one of Bert's visits to the hospital. Bert told him he was going to have to turn down the job because two months was too long to leave the ranch. We're too small an outfit to have a foreman. And Paul volunteered to run things for us, just like that. He's kind of impulsive, you know.'

'Oh, really?' Jenny said innocently.

Peg's tongue emerged from the corner of her mouth while she strained the cherries, and reserved the juice in a bowl. 'At first we told him we wouldn't dream of imposing on him like that. But he really seemed to be looking forward to it. And he can be very persuasive when he wants to be.'

'Can he ever!' Jenny murmured wryly to herself.

'Pardon?'

'Oh—I said he's also, er, clever.'

Peg looked at her oddly, then went on to mix the juice with a little sugar and cornstarch, and poured it into a pan. 'Actually, Bert thinks Paul's willing to stay because he got more knocked around in that crash than he's admitting, and he needs to recuperate.'

Jenny glanced up sharply from the coffee she was measuring. 'Do you—do you think that's really true?'

Peg's arched eyebrows set her at ease. 'Are you kidding? A little thing like a plane crash, slow Paul Brant down? Forget it.' She lowered her voice. 'If you want my opinion, you're the main reason he's so willing to stick around here.'

'Me?' Jenny looked up with a startled jerk. 'But we hardly know each other!'

Peg gave a gravelly chuckle. 'Maybe, but I've been watching him, and he looks at you like he'd sure like to know you better.' She stopped what she was doing for a moment and looked at Jenny with candid, friendly eyes. 'And to tell you the truth, I hope you *are* the reason.'

'Oh, no, I couldn't be!' Jenny shook her head vigorously while she tried to think of what else to say. 'Oh, I think he likes me at the moment, all right—or rather, he's attracted to me. But I can't imagine holding his interest for two weeks, let alone two months.'

'Well now, I'm not so sure about that. Maybe if you——'

'Not that I want to,' Jenny added hastily.

Peg sighed heavily, her matchmaking unproductive. 'Too bad. If you ask me, you'd be perfect for him. You ought to see those simpering little sex kittens that usually hang around him, with their glamour-girl——' It was her turn to be embarrassed. 'I didn't mean you're not attractive; far from it. I just meant——'

'Don't worry about it,' Jenny said with a smile. 'I know what you mean.'

She went on calmly making the coffee, but her mind had seized eagerly on what Peg had said. Was it really possible that she was perfect for him? Peg knew him well, after all; knew the kind of man he was, the kind of needs he had . . . She caught herself abruptly before she went any further. That wasn't the question at all. The question was whether he was perfect for *her*. And the answer was a resounding no—even if, she admitted frankly to herself, he did seem to meet certain needs *she* had.

'You really wouldn't want to wish him on me, would you?' she asked, working to keep her tone light and unconcerned. 'Paul's the most reckless man I've ever met, and I'd hate to be contemplating widow-hood before I even got married.'

Peg laughed. 'You've definitely got a point there, but men change, you know.' She looked up from the glistening cherry sauce she was stirring, her good-humoured face suddenly serious. 'Paul wasn't always

so cavalier about risking his neck. He'd never admit it
to anyone—and he'd strangle me if he knew I told you
this—but the real reasons he's like that is——'

Jenny groaned inwardly when the thump of the
kitchen door opening interrupted Peg. Why did the
men have to come barging in to open the drinks
cabinet just when things were getting interesting?

Watching Paul amiably argue with his friend over
the merits of Remy Martin versus Courvoisier, Jenny
tried to convince herself that it was just as well that
her curiosity remained unsatisfied. Knowing more
about him might stir compassion and understanding—two elements that can cut through the most
armoured of hearts, and she had barely begun forging
a shell against him.

Peg had completed the dessert by the time a brandy
was selected and Jenny had no chance to renew her
private chat with Peg in the kitchen. And then the
evening faded away in friendly talk and laughter,
and, by the time they'd finished their last refills of
coffee, it was time to go.

'You made quite a hit with Peg and Bert,' Paul said as
the door closed behind them. 'I thought you would.'

'I like them, too,' she said, wishing uneasily that he
would move a little further away. With him gently
taking her arm as they walked down the porch steps,
and with his clean, masculine scent blending with the
cool, juniper-laden night air, his closeness had her
heart trembling in her throat. How could the simple,
ordinary touch of fingertips through several layers of
clothing be so incredibly, shudderingly electrifying?

And if he could do that by brushing her *elbow* . . .!

Did he feel it, too? She doubted it. As they began to walk down the gravelled path he let his hand fall away from her arm as if he hadn't even been aware that it was there.

'You know, you just might be the most unpredictable, unpigeonholeable woman I've ever met.'

'Oh? Just what's so unpredictable about me?' she asked coolly. 'Is there something wrong with my outfit?'

She had seen how unmistakably flabbergasted he'd been when, only a few hours after he had seen her looking like a bedraggled, soap-spattered tomboy, she'd walked in looking like a model—if she did say so herself. And if she had to coax him a little to hear him admit it, it was worth it.

Jenny wasn't usually the sort of person who fished for compliments, and she got what she deserved—a simple, amused lifting of his eyebrows.

'Your outfit? No, but I can't quite figure out whether you're playing games with me or not,' he said, gazing up into the starry night. 'I thought you were bluffing this morning when you said you could spend weeks around me without—what was it?—without so much as a flutter of the pulse.' He looked back down at her, his head cocked. 'Now I'm not so sure,' he continued thoughtfully. 'You're more sophisticated than I thought. I just might have to do some reassessment.'

Which went to show the power of the right clothes, whether Paul was aware of them or not, Jenny reflected ruefully. He'd reassess his reassessment pretty quickly if he knew about the butterflies palpitating in her stomach.

'And does that disappoint you?' she asked warily.

'Not a bit,' he said calmly. 'I prefer my women complex.'

'*Your* women?' Jenny halted abruptly, her irritaion sparked by his easy arrogance. 'Do you really think you can drop into a woman's life out of the blue and sweep her off her feet just by looking at her twice?' She stifled the unbidden thought that that was exactly what he *had* done, only never mind the 'twice'. 'Why——'

He stopped her by holding two fingers gently to her lips. 'Stick to the subject. We're not talking about *any* woman. We're talking about you,' he said, and moved his hand so that the backs of his fingers softly stroked her cheek. She held her breath. 'Jenny,' he said, his voice a throaty whisper, 'has it occurred to you there are other things besides sparring that two people could be doing on a warm, starry night—far more pleasant things?'

Jenny fought down the impulse to agree and the stronger impulse to melt right into his arms on the spot. Instead, she closed her eyes—she doubted if he could see her face in the darkness—and took a deep, steadying breath, trying to find her bearings, fighting against the seductive caress of his fingers against her cheek.

The crisp, desert starlight was brighter than she realised, bright enough for Paul to see her eyelids closed and trembling, her chin tilted up in that provocative, pugnacious way that always pleased him and made the laughter tremble just behind his lips. Her soft hair stirred in the desert night wind, brushing the back of his hand, and he felt a warm stirring in himself, as if in response. Without thinking, he moved half a step closer, then caught himself as her eyes opened.

'I'll admit no such thing,' she said, trying to ignore the hand that still lay against her cheek, now gently moving to explore the line of her jaw, the tender flesh of her throat. 'I don't . . . I mean, I'm not interested in . . .' She groped wildly for words to disperse the electricity in the air. 'Paul, it's late and I just want to go home.'

She heard something close to panic in her own voice, and she tossed her head to escape his hand and began to turn away. But he merely dropped his hand to her upper arm, and grasped her other arm as well. For a moment he simply looked at her, his face as set and unreadable as a marble statue's in the moonlight. Then, slowly, deliberately, he pulled her to him.

She wasn't naïve enough to be caught off guard, of course, and she stiffened her muscles to resist him. But the relentless, masculine power of his hands, and then the thrilling, shocking surge of feeling that exploded at her very centre when he pressed her into the long, lean length of him, turned her will to jelly.

'Paul . . .' she murmured, not knowing what she wanted to say, not even aware that she'd spoken. 'Paul . . .'

His face was above hers, his eyes shadowed and invisible. In the starlight she saw a muscle tense at his temple, and then his face bent slowly, inexorably to hers.

Her own face rose to meet it, numbly it seemed to her, but the touch of his lips was like a jolt of electricity that arched her back and pushed her upward against him. The rest of the world vanished.

There was nothing else but Paul, nothing but his
burning mouth, his heated, thrusting body, nothing
but the exquisite, torturing hunger that ravished and
consumed her.

Her fingers dug convulsively into the powerful
muscles of his back—when had her arms circled
around him? Paul groaned and wrapped his arms
even more tightly around her, gathering her into him
with a growing force that had to crush her if he didn't
stop. Bewildered, frightened, ecstatic, she didn't know
whether it was pain or joy she felt. And she certainly
didn't care.

But a part of her *did* care. Somewhere inside, a tiny,
urgent voice—all that was left of her will-power and
her good sense—was whispering warnings, or trying
to. Pain, that was what it was, the small voice insisted;
pain, and confusion, and doubt. And they were
nothing to what she'd feel if she were foolish enough to
succumb to an entanglement—a purely physical,
utterly sexual entanglement—that could only lead to
misery.

He was an eagle, remember, the voice cautioned,
and she was a mere hummingbird. When Paul
released her slightly, and started moving his hands
tantalisingly up over her ribcage towards her breasts,
the nagging warnings finally took hold, and with no
time to spare. It didn't take much knowledge of men to
understand that Paul Brant was in the 'fish-or-cut-
bait' category. He would have a low tolerance for
sexual game-playing.

Jenny put her hands on his chest and pushed away
from him. To her surprise he held firm only for a

moment. Then his hands dropped to his sides and he took a step back.

'I guess I asked for that,' she said raggedly, her breath coming in deep, starved gasps. Not that he was breathing any better. 'But it's not going to happen again.'

Even in the dark she was aware of the burning intensity of his eyes. It was almost as if they were lasers, cutting through every defence she'd thrown up, and searing her very centre.

'Don't be so sure,' he said huskily.

'But I am,' she said, her confidence growing as his gaze cooled. 'All right, I admit I'm physically attracted to you, but that's all, and I ... I deplore meaningless sex.'

'I see. And sex between us could only be meaningless, of course.' His voice was taunting now.

This was no time to mince words. 'Yes,' she said with a great deal more certainty than she felt. 'Do you know why you're attracted to me?'

'Because life is always so peaceful around you?'

'I'm trying to be serious,' she snapped. 'It's because——'

'——I enjoy your lectures so much?'

It felt good to be getting annoyed with him. Or at least, it felt a lot safer than what she'd been feeling. 'No,' she said briskly. 'You're attracted, one, because of the dramatic way we met; two, because I suppose you think I'm not too bad-looking; three, because you think I have a few unusual qualities, and——'

'It seems to me that you've been giving this meaningless physical attraction of ours a lot of thought.'

'——and I'm undoubtedly attracted—slightly—to you for exactly the same reasons,' she continued, undeterred. She was doing too well to let him throw her off the track. 'Pardon the cliché, but I'm sure that in our case, familiarity would only breed contempt. I'm a wet blanket, remember?'

'How could I forget?' he said, not in words but with the tilt of his head.

'And you,' she went on, her irritation growing very satisfactorily, 'are nothing but a reckless, devil-may-care——' She stopped herself. On second thoughts, the last thing she wanted was to anger him. Her shoulders, her mouth, most of her body still burned with the sheer male strength of him. She struggled to find a polite word. '. . . devil-may-care . . .'

'Adventurer?' he suggested blandly.

'Yes. Thank you. That will do nicely.'

She turned to walk the rest of the distance to her car, but he stopped her again with a hand on her arm. She froze.

'And as long as I stick around this remote backwater,' he drawled, 'you intend to keep those baser instincts of yours under very tight control. So if I'm in the mood for meaningless sex, I'd better look somewhere else.' His voice, so urbane, so infuriatingly self-possessed, poked great, jagged holes in her barely maintained equilibrium. 'Is that what you're telling me?'

'Precisely,' she snapped, tilting her chin firmly upward. 'And now will you let go of me? I really do want to go home.'

'There's just one small problem that I can see with

your theory,' he said, his hand remaining very firmly where it was.

'Only one?' she said drily, wondering if he had any idea of the melting potency of his powerful hand on her arm.

'It's simply that we're not as different as you'd like to think. I was watching you pretty closely yesterday down on that ledge, and I saw how you jumped at the chance to cross over the traverse with that stretcher.' He smiled confidently, his teeth white in the starlight.

My God, she thought, I'm in trouble. When did I ever find a man's *teeth* sexy before?

'Sure,' he went on, 'you channel your need for risk-taking into rescue work, but you're as much of an adventurer as I am, Jenny, and if you were honest you'd admit it to yourself, instead of ranting at me.'

'*Ranting!*' She set her jaw, grateful again for the surge of anger. If he kept managing to infuriate her with every other sentence, maybe she would still be all right. 'Thank you for *your* lecture, and now, if you'd be kind enough to let go of me . . .'

'With pleasure.' His hand fell away. 'There's just one more thing.'

Jenny stood her ground. 'And that is?'

He grinned and folded his arms. 'That only time can tell exactly what familiarity is going to breed.'

By the time Jenny had driven past the sign announcing Cochise Bend's city limits, she had gone a long way towards collecting her wits again. As Peg had said, Paul wasn't the kind of person to stay very long in any one place. All she had to do was to figure out some way of resisting—for two measly months— that combination of clean good looks, self-assured masculine power, and—what was the point of denying it?—raw sexuality that radiated from him like warmth from a heater. He was quite a man, Paul Brant; the most damnably attractive man she'd ever met. But he wasn't the man for her, and if she fooled herself into thinking he was, there would be bad times ahead.

No, she would simply have to work out a way to keep her distance, physical and mental. And the way to start was obvious: not to accept any more dates, do her level best to avoid being alone with him, and most important of all, stop thinking so darn much about him!

Starting right now. She pulled into her garage, switched off the engine, and resolutely pushed Paul Brant from her mind.

CHAPTER SIX

ON SUNDAY mornings Jenny usually awarded herself the luxury of sleeping well into the morning before attacking her weekly house-cleaning chores. It hardly surprised her, though, to find herself wide awake before dawn the Sunday after dinner at the Lathans. The night hadn't brought much in the way of rest. It was a great deal easier to push Paul out of her mind than it was to keep him out.

She glanced at the silent emergency beeper on the bedside table. This was one morning when she could use a major distraction. Why was it that people never got into trouble at convenient times? A sudden, moody smile played around her lips. She had forgotten for a moment that Paul was a member of the team now, and a call-up would just throw them together. Until he went his merry, uncaring way to stir up some other poor female's life, her avocation wasn't going to provide much in the way of escape.

Which reminded her; there was something she needed to talk to one of the other team members about. She had begun to dial the number before she realised that Sue Bonner would hardly appreciate a telephone call at six o'clock on a Sunday morning! Jenny sighed, remembering the days when she too could doze away whole mornings with unclouded mind and untroubled spirit. Oh, well, there wasn't anything that said one had to wait until nine o'clock to make a start on spring-cleaning.

Three hours later, with the barest of starts made—how in the world had the windows got into that state?—she made her telephone call to Sue, and with some satisfaction, replaced the receiver in its cradle. The moment she did, her own telephone rang, making her start.

She let it ring twice more while she took a long, deep breath to quiet herself. Somehow, she had no doubt about who it was.

'Jenny?'

She was right, of course. 'Yes,' she said, quite calmly, considering that the thumping of her heart was as loud as the voice in her ear. 'Who is this?' No sense letting him know the state she was in.

'Paul.' When she didn't say anything he said, 'Paul Brant? Perhaps you remember me?'

'Oh, yes, vaguely,' she said, her voice satisfactorily cool. This wasn't going badly at all. 'What can I do for you?'

'What *we* can do is set up my next training session. You fled before we could get around to it last night.'

'I most certainly did not *flee* . . . but I did forget. I had a lot on my mind——'

'I'll say you did,' he cut in, and she had no trouble seeing the grin on his face.

She hadn't known before that people could blush when they talked on the telephone, but she knew it now. 'I didn't mean that——' she said quickly.

'Mean what?' he asked innocently.

'I didn't mean . . . that is, I was talking about

problems at work, and—and——' What was the use?
As usual, it had taken him all of thirty seconds to
reduce her to adolescent incoherence. She sighed.
'How about next Saturday? All day, if possible.
There's a lot we have to cover.'

She winced at her own words and steeled herself for
however he was going to twist them, but he surprised
her and only laughed. Maybe she was so easy to
disconcert that the challenge was going out of it for
him.

'Saturday's fine,' he said. 'Tell me, do I get
promoted from washing the truck to polishing the
chrome?'

Jenny laughed, too. 'No, it's time to get you started
on terrain familiarisation. By hiking the local trails
you keep abreast of the hazards—washouts, rock
slides, that kind of thing—and you start to get a feel
for where a person's likely to get lost.'

'Makes sense. Look, if it's an all-day thing,' he said
smoothly, 'suppose I bring a picnic lunch for us?'

'Good idea.' Jenny congratulated herself on how
well she had anticipated this conversation. 'But you'd
better make it for three. Sue Bonner's going to be with
us. She's that grey-haired, sort of motherly woman on
the team.'

He chuckled. 'A chaperon. Well, it figures.'

'She's not a chaperon,' Jenny rejoined. 'It's just
that it's as important for you to get to know the team
members as the geographical area.'

Paul's 'Hmm' dripped with scepticism, but before
he could press the point she told him the meting time,
said a quick goodbye, and hung up.

Afterwards, she stood for a moment with her hand on the telephone. It seemed as if she were incapable of carrying through the simplest of schemes without his seeing through them in seconds. Darn the man for making her resort to scheming in the first place!

Angrily, she picked up a cloth and got vigorously back to cleaning windows, but the burst of exasperation with him hadn't even played itself out before she felt the mounting warmth of excitement over the prospect of a whole day's hiking with him—chaperon or no chaperon. Her window-wiping came to a slow, lazy stop as she found herself gazing dreamily out into the street, a vacant smile on her face. All day in the fresh air, in the lovely Chiricahuas, with Paul Conan Brant! She shivered with pleasure, and then mentally kicked herself and got back to the windows even more energetically. Just what was it she wanted, anyway? She couldn't keep it straight in her mind from one minute to the next. Nobody had to tell her, she thought grimly; she was her own worst enemy. Paul was just a distant second.

The following week seemed to last for ever, despite the fact that she stayed busy both in the bank and out of it. Partly it was because she couldn't keep herself from looking up expectantly every time the bank door swung open, and catching her breath whenever the phone rang. And when it turned out to be someone else, as it always did, and disappointment washed over her, she would force herself to sit still and listen to a self-delivered, five-minute scolding.

But it was also a useful week, a week in which she'd learned something about herself and came to some important conclusions. And, in a way, Paul was responsible. His explosive intrusion into her life had done more than stir up the long-hidden emotional side of her; it had also sparked the vivacity and zest for life that had been dormant so very long. Oh, he had definitely exaggerated when he said she was no less an adventurer than he was, but he did have a point. As the week progressed, she began to understand that this comfortable, routine job of hers provided her with more than a practical way of supporting herself. It had been her haven of order, security, and predictability all these years, when—except on rescue missions—she had rigidly suppressed her natural need for challenge, excitement, and—well—adventure.

The job had disciplined and matured her, too, and for that she was grateful. Clearly, though, it was getting to be time to leave havens behind and get on with finding a career that meant more to her than safety. There were all sorts of interesting things she might be good at. Once, she'd wanted more than anything else to be a national park ranger. Well, why *couldn't* she? She was ready to go back to school if she had to, and more than willing to start at the bottom. By Friday she had decided to do it. She spent her lunch hour at Cochise Community College talking to a counsellor, and by the time it was done, to her own surprise, she had tentatively signed up for two evening forestry courses in the autumn.

That was a long time away, but maybe it was all to the good. She had a more pressing personal problem that she had to deal with first!

*   *   *

Jenny was humming to herself at the kitchen sink, filling her canteen with water for the hike when the doorbell rang.

'Hi, Sue,' she said with a grin. 'Be with you in——' Her eyes widened. 'You're—you're wearing a skirt . . . and *heels*! How can you possibly hike through——'

'I can't come.' Sue spread her hands apologetically. Jenny froze with dismay. 'Oh, no!'

'Oh, yes.' Sue's lips turned down at the corners. 'My niece just called me. She woke up with the 'flu and her husband's away on a business trip. I've got to go over and help with her kids.'

'Why don't you bring them along?' Jenny suggested hopefully. 'They'd probably love it. We don't really have to go all the way up to the top of Good Peak, you know. We could cut the hike down.'

Sue laughed and shook her head. 'You'd have to cut it down a heck of a lot. Mike's two and half, and Jeffy's six weeks.'

Biting her lower lip, Jenny contemplated offering to switch places—two babies and a few 'flu germs sounded a lot less hazardous than a long day off in the wilds in Paul's company, without the comforting presence of a third party. She sighed; no, that wouldn't work. She had made such a to-do with Jake about taking on Paul's training, that she couldn't very well back out of it now.

After Sue left, Jenny frowningly finished filling up her canteen, then cleared away the breakfast dishes, wondering all the while just how she was going to deal with this tricky new development. If Paul—she realised suddenly that he was half an hour late. He had said he would come at eight sharp, and it was eight-thirty. Where in the world was he? How thoughtless of him. If he were going to be this late, the least he might have done would have been to call. He's probably simply forgotten about it, she thought angrily. No doubt he had too many more important things——

Jenny burst out laughing at herself. Thirty seconds ago she'd been practically chewing her nails with anxiety over having to spend the day with him, and now she was irritated because he had failed to come! Being involved with Paul Brant had a lot in common with being a yo-yo. Up one minute and down the next, with Paul somehow managing to jerk the string even when he wasn't there.

The harsh sound of a car pulling abruptly into the driveway and stopping with a jerk cut short all thoughts of yo-yos. It was the white Porsche all right. Why, she asked herself, hadn't she used the extra half-hour to line up another team member, instead of simply moping around? Well, too late now. She squared her shoulders, lifted her chin, and went to the door.

And was astonished at the smouldering fury in Paul's face.

'Paul—what's the——'

'Where's your friend?' he cut in icily, looking over her shoulder into the empty living-room.

Jenny drew back involuntarily. Was it her he was angry at? But why?

'Sue?' she ventured. 'She wasn't able to make it. At the last minute——'

'We'll take my car, then.' With an impatient movement he took her pack from her hand and turned away.

She had to walk quickly to keep up with him. After tossing her things into the boot, he thrust her into the seat—not very much more gently—and grimly slammed the door.

When they reached the outskirts of Cochise Bend without him having said a word, Jenny stole a nervous glance at his forbidding profile.

'Somehow,' she said, 'I'm getting the impression I may have done something to annoy you—something more than usual, that is.'

'You might say that,' he answered shortly.

When he failed to elaborate, her own temper started simmering. Why, he hadn't even apologised for being late! And what could he have to be angry about, anyway. Well, if he wanted to keep it to himself and stew in his own juices, that was fine with her. She stared coldly ahead, and they didn't speak again until they got to the intersection with Highway Eighty.

'Which way?' he asked, without looking at her.

'East,' she said shortly, not to be outdone for curtness. But then she relented; Paul's being rude was hardly a reason to follow suit.

'I thought we'd start with the most popular trail inside the Coronado National Forest boundary,' she added crisply. Being polite didn't mean she couldn't be all business. 'We're always called out there two or three times a year to help the rangers find lost hikers.'

'Doesn't say much for their trails.'

Jenny bridled at his sardonic tone. The fact that he

was nursing some imaginary grievance didn't give him the right to take it out on the Forest Service personnel—who maintained the trails excellently, as a matter of fact.

'Their trails are fine,' she retorted glacially. 'It's the ridiculous people who go wandering off the path without taking the most ordinary precautions—such as having a map or a compass.' She was working up an invigorating head of steam, and for good measure she went on, 'Just the way there are ridiculous people who ask for trouble by flying off in ultralights when they don't know how to handle them.'

'And ridiculous women,' Paul shot back scathingly, 'who ask for trouble by wandering off alone on the streets at night.'

Bewildered, Jenny stared at him. 'What?'

'You heard me.' He glanced at her briefly. 'Or don't tell me you moved in the last couple of weeks?'

'Paul,' she said blankly, 'what are you talking about?'

'About the fact,' he ground out, his lips compressed into a straight, thin line, 'that when I walked you home after dinner at the Copper King, we wound up in front of a door all of two blocks from the hotel.' His voice grew more heated. 'But when I showed up there today, the man who owns the house—who wasn't too keen on being dragged out of bed at eight o'clock on a Saturday morning by the way—couldn't seem to recollect your living there.'

He glared fiercely at her with cold green eyes that seemed to bore through her. '*That* is what I'm talking about!'

Jenny managed to stifle an urge to gulp, but the heat in her cheeks told her that she had been less successful in keeping herself from blushing. 'Oh, dear,' she mumbled, 'I'd forgotten all about that. No wonder you said you knew how to get to my apartment. I thought—I don't know what I thought.' She tried a timid grin. 'And that's why you were late?'

Paul wasn't the type who melted at a timid grin. 'Yes, damn it,' he muttered, 'that's why I was late, but don't change the subject. I want an explanation.'

Jenny now permitted herself to take that gulp. 'Sure,' she said gamely. 'To begin with, you have a big-city mentality about crime. Cochise Bend isn't New York; it's a small town. A woman can feel perfectly safe on the street at night—so I wasn't doing anything dangerous at all.'

He considered her words, and—surprisingly—seemed a little mollified by them. 'OK,' he said slowly, 'you're basically right; I can see that. But still, you never know——'

'Honestly,' she interrupted, laughing, 'I'm having a hard time believing that the international daredevil I helped pull out of a flimsy flying machine in the Chiricahuas is actually sitting there with a straight face, giving *me* a lecture on safety!'

She watched the set, grim displeasure of his face ease almost unwillingly, and then, suddenly, he was laughing too. 'Well,' he said, 'I admit you do have something of a point.'

She sank back against the car seat, relieved. 'Of course I do,' she said, 'it's not as if——'

'But I'm still waiting for an explanation.' His voice

wasn't quite as bleak as it had been before, but there was still a no-nonsense ring to it.

She nodded. 'Of why I told you we'd reached my place when we hadn't?'

'Yes,' he said drily, 'that little matter.'

She sighed. This seemed like a time for telling it the way it was. 'If,' she said, 'you'll cast your mind back to our walk, I think you'll remember that you weren't being the most gentlemanly of companions——'

'Come on,' he flared, 'I didn't do anything you didn't want me to do, down deep. When I kissed you——'

'I wasn't talking about that,' she said hurriedly. 'I mean, not only about that.' Darn it, there was that hot rush of blood to her cheeks again. What a give-away her face was! 'You were overbearing, and rude,' she went on warmly, knowing that the best defence was a merciless offence, 'and I didn't particularly appreciate being called names.'

It was his turn to be astonished. 'Names! What are you——'

'Well, there was "wet blanket" for one . . .'

'Oh, sure, but I was just——'

'And "prude", and "pill", and ——'

'Oh, yeah,' he said sheepishly, 'I forgot. I guess I wasn't being at my most charming, was I?'

But she wasn't about to let up, now that she had him on the run. 'And "prig",' she continued, 'and let's see, there was something else, but I can't quite——'

'"Drip",' he supplied, and took his eyes off the road long enough to give her a wry little grin.

Her answering smile relaxed what was left of the

tension between them, and suddenly the whole thing seemed so funny that they laughed until the tears came.

'Do you always pick up this many rocks,' Paul asked, his green eyes flickering with humour, 'or is it just that you want to have something handy to brain me with if I step out of line?'

Jenny laughed. Surprising as it was, the possibility of Paul's stepping out of line couldn't have been further from her mind. She had been a little uneasy at first, but within minutes of starting the winding, climbing trail to the fire tower on Goat Peak, they were deep in entertaining but safely impersonal conversation.

He had been genuinely fascinated by the dramatic shifts in temperature, vegetation and wildlife as they had gained in altitude, and she'd told him that the Chiricahua Mountains were sometimes called the 'Sky Islands' because they floated like cool, Alpine islands above the vast, golden sea that was the Sonora Desert. Walking up into them was like climbing a vertical climate ladder, with interesting new rungs every few hundred feet.

Soon they had been chatting comfortably about everything from troublesome insects (that got less troublesome the higher they went), to wild flowers, to glacial periods, to the Indians who had given so many of the local places their names. When she hadn't been stopping to catch her breath, that was. Not Paul. He never even seemed to breathe hard, as if a hike that climbed 3,000 feet in five miles was just an everyday stroll. One more thing to be annoyed with about this infuriating man. He had been laid up in the hospital just a couple of weeks ago, he never took any exercise as far as she knew, he ate the richest foods imaginable and drank more than was good for him . . . and he was in better shape than she was! How irritating!

But by the time they'd reached the top of the forested peak her temper had vanished. The air was too clear, the view too grand, the pines too aromatic— and Paul too guilelessly charming—for her to stay annoyed. They had found a protected spot out of the breeze and unpacked the lunch of cold herbed chicken and vegetable salad that Paul had brought. It had looked like far too much to eat, but somehow they had managed to eat not only their own portions but most of Sue's as well. Now they were sipping coffee and munching the home-made chocolate chip cookies that were Jenny's contribution. And with her free hand she was toying with a sharp-edged piece of granite flecked with mica.

'No, I'm not planning to brain you,' Jenny said. 'Not that I won't, if there's a good reason to.'

He smiled lazily, too contentedly full of coffee and chicken to take her seriously.

She was feeling lazy too, and leaned back against the satisfying roughness of a thick old pine tree. 'I guess I do pick up a lot of rocks,' she said, tossing away the hunk of granite and brushing her dusty hand against her jeans. 'It's a habit I picked up from my father. Dad was quite a rockhound.'

'Was.'

'Yes, he died three years ago.'

'I'm sorry. Did you used to go rock-hunting with him?'

She smiled, remembering. 'The rocks were just a bonus. What we did was go prospecting. We must have spent every other weekend when I was growing up, wandering around the mountains, looking for the gold strike that would make us rich. When we found it he was going to quit working as a heavy equipment operator at the mine, and we'd all live in luxury for the rest of our lives.'

'Ever find any?'

'The closest we ever came was huge pile of iron pyrite.'

'Iron pyrite?'

'"Fool's gold". It looks like the real thing, but it's worthless.'

'Disappointing. Still it must have been fun for a kid,' he said with something like wistfulness in his voice, 'prospecting in the mountains with your father.'

'It was wonderful.' She settled back more comfortably against the tree, the plastic cup cradled in both hands, and—hesitantly at first, and then more spiritedly when she saw he was really interested—she told him about how it had been.

About the long, lovely, dusty hikes, about sleeping under those incredible night skies, with the stars glittering and dancing like rivers of diamonds. About the mouth-watering aroma of the beef stew Mom used to make over the camp-fires. About the time her sister Gail got lost in Battle Rock Cave for six hours, and then hid from them because she had been afraid Mom

would spank her for tearing her shirt. About how cold
it was waking up in her sleeping-bag in the morning,
and how Mom would let her have just a few drops of
coffee in her hot, sugared milk, just to help her get her
blood circulating again.

'I think that's why I love coffee so much,' she said
with a smile. 'All I have to do is taste it and I can smell
the cold mountain air . . .' She sat up with a start. 'My
gosh, how long have I been talking?'

Paul was lying full length on the pine needles, his
shoulders against a smooth boulder a few feet from
her, his empty coffee cup propped on his chest. He
took his eyes off the cotton-wool white clouds
scudding across the blue sky and looked at his watch.
'Three-quarters of an hour, give or take a few
minutes.'

'Three-quarters . . .!'

Once she'd begun to talk, he had prompted her
with nods or simple grunts of understanding, and she
had gone on, and on, and on. It had been a kind of
sweet release for her to go wandering among those
gentle old memories with Paul at her side, so to speak.
She hadn't known it was possible to feel so relaxed, so
unguarded in his presence. Still, three-quarters of an
hour? Was it possible?

'I hope I haven't bored you,' she said with a smile.

'Not a bit.'

She finished the last of her coffee, which was cold
by now, and set the cup down beside her. 'What about
you? What was your childhood like? Didn't I read
somewhere that your father was an Air Force colonel?

You must have done a lot of travelling even before you were grown.'

Live clams were not to be found in Arizona, so Jenny had no idea of what they looked like when they snapped their shells closed. She suspected, though, that Paul's sudden change of expression was a reasonably close approximation.

'Quite a bit,' he said brusquely, 'but I won't bore you with the details. Pretty dull stuff.'

Her cheeks grew abruptly warm. If he called his own exotic background dull, what must he be thinking about the humdrum history of Jenny Roberts? Why had she gone on like that? Why had he let her? She turned quickly away from him, using the excuse of getting to her feet and brushing the pine needles from her, and began to pack away the debris from their picnic. She groped for a change of subject.

'Have you heard from Peg and Bert since they've left?' she asked as offhandedly as she could.

A wave of acute disappointment swept over her when he readily picked up her conversational lead. No volunteered information about his past, no more questions about hers. The subject was dropped. He couldn't have cared less about really getting to know her. How could she have deluded herself the way she had? Those hadn't been grunts of understanding, they'd been snores!

Unexpected tears stung the backs of her eyelids, and with an effort she blinked them away, trying not to sniffle. It took her a few moments to make head or tail of what he was talking about; he'd obviously answered her question and then gone on to something else. When she did understand, she was surprised and pleased. He was telling her about a call he had received from an old college friend he hadn't seen in almost a decade.

'Peter said he heard through the search-and-rescue grapevine that I'd joined the team here and he wanted to welcome me into the fraternity.' He smiled. 'Why is everybody so amazed to hear that I'm doing something useful?'

Jenny thought she would pass that one up. 'Which team does your friend work for?'

'Sierra Madre. In California.'

'Do you mean Peter MacCabe?' Jenny exclaimed. 'Is he a friend of yours?'

'An old friend.' He lifted an eyebrow. 'Do you know him?'

'I wish I did. I just know some of the papers he's written on avalanche rescue. He's really good.'

'Well, you're going to get your wish,' Paul said, getting lazily to his feet. 'Peter's running a weekend training session at the end of the month—in avalanche rescue, as a matter of fact. I figured you'd be interested, so I wangled an invitation for you.'

Jenny perked up at once. 'Really? A course from Peter MacCabe? That's wonderful! Here in Arizona?' she asked with enthusiasm, and then fought down a wild urge to laugh.

This was ridiculous. There she was, bouncing like a Yo-yo again. He'd jerked her from gentle tranquillity, to humiliation, to disappointment, to surpise and pleasure, to enthusiasm—all in not much more than sixty seconds. And as she knew only too well, that was only the beginning of what he could so easily arouse in her. Despite the slightly hysterical laughter aching for release at the back of her throat, it was no laughing matter; her emotional resilience would be worn to a paper-thin frazzle if this kept up. She was going to have to do something about it.

And she would. As soon as she figured out what.

'No,' Paul said, 'it's going to be in California, in the Sierras, about two hundred miles from LA.'

'LA?' She stared at him blankly. He was getting her confused with his jet-set friends. Did he really think she could afford to go flying off to California whenever she felt like it?

He picked up his backpack and shrugged into it, then grinned. 'No need to thank me so profusely.'

'No, I appreciate it. It's just—well, it may be a problem getting there.'

'Why? We'll fly out Friday afternoon and be there by evening. What's the problem? You can get a couple of hours off at the bank, can't you.'

She continued to stare at him. 'We?'

'Naturally. I got us both invited. We can go together.'

'That sounds nice,' she said, thinking what a different world he came from and wondering what it would feel like to be a part of it. 'I'm sorry, but the problem isn't transportation; it's how to pay for it. I've just got new curtains for my living-room, and my——'

'Jenny,' he said drily, 'I wasn't planning on charging you for a ride in my plane.'

'——credit card account is as close to its limit as

I ... You have an airplane?'

He nodded. 'Sure, a Learjet. At the Vista airstrip. That's how I usually get around.'

'But the Porsche?'

'Rented. That's just for local travel.'

'Oh!' Different world was an understatement. She might have guessed Paul had a jet of his own if she'd thought about it, but could you really rent a *Porsche*? Not in Cochise Bend, she was sure of that!

She surprised him by bursting into laughter as they started down the trail together. It looked as if she was going to get at least a taste of his world, because this was one opportunity she couldn't bring herself to pass up. After all, they would probably never be alone with each other except when they were in the air—and he would have his mind fully occupied then.

'All right,' she said, 'I'd love to go, then. And thanks for getting me invited.'

His eyes twinkled in response. 'Would I go anywhere without my trainer?'

'*Trainer!*' Jenny scoffed. 'You've hardly needed one. And you absorbed all the information in those handbooks in a week.'

He raised his eyebrows in a sardonic response. 'Surely my ears deceive me. For a moment there, I actually thought I was being complimented on my diligence.'

She laughed. 'Paul, may I ask you a question?'

He cocked his head, his eyes intent on her face, and suddenly her pulse was racing again. She looked quickly away.

'Why are you putting all this energy and effort into

joining the team for such a little while?'

'What makes you think it's only for a little while?' he countered.

'Well, the Lathans will only be gone for two months.' She shrugged. 'And you won't be staying beyond then, will you?' At his silence she turned suddenly to him. '. . . Will you?'

'It depends.'

'On?' Her voice was tight in her throat. One more bounce of the yo-yo.

'On whether or not I find a piece of property that suits me. I've been looking. I wouldn't want to spend my summers in Arizona, but I've started to think the winters might be fun.' He smiled lazily at her. 'What do you think of the idea?'

Jenny almost stopped in her tracks. Dazedly, she willed her legs to keep moving down the rocky trail. This was the last thing she needed! With any luck she might keep herself from falling in love with him for two months, but if he were to *live* here . . .? She was already more than half in love with him and it hadn't even been *one* month!

'Well, I don't know,' she said, trying to sound as if she were treating it as a casual question. 'It's pretty quiet around here. I should think you'd get bored pretty quickly.'

His glance narrowed. He made no effort to hide his amusement, and she quailed at how easily he saw through her.

'On the contrary, it's extremely challenging,' he said with a sardonic glint in his green eyes. 'I haven't felt this stimulated in years.'

'I hope you keep feeling that way when you get your first call-up at three in the morning,' she retorted, pretending to misunderstand him—which wasn't easy, considering how his eyes were devouring hers. A wash of colour rose on her cheeks in spite of herself.

'*That*'s going to depend on what it was I was doing at the time,' he said, smiling wickedly. 'You never know.'

'Oh, that reminds me,' she said, refusing to be drawn on to dangerous grounds, 'I can arrange for you to take your first field test next weekend if you like.'

'Fine,' Paul said. 'How many chaperons do we get for that one? The whole team?'

For the first time in a while, she looked him squarely in the eye.

'You'd better believe it!' she said with feeling.

But there wasn't time for Paul's field test the following weekend. Jenny had forgotten that it was the beginning of spring vacation, which, as usual, brought out hordes of hikers and campers. That would have been bad enough, but on Friday night a freak blizzard blanketed the Southwest and brought with it a numbing cold front that gave the team its most active and exhausting week in three years.

On Saturday morning before it was light, they started after two hikers in the Chiricahuas, a young married couple who had failed to return to Turkey Creek camp ground in the evening after what was to have been an afternoon walk. The team fanned out along the nearby trails, and it was Jake who came across them, frozen to death, less than a mile from the camp and its life-giving warmth. It was a distressing beginning to an interminable week: rescuing stranded climbers ill-prepared for the weather; searching for fair-weather hikers who knew little about protecting themselves from the cold; looking for the pilots of not one but two small planes that had been lost in the mountains.

What made it even worse was that there was little trained outside help. The police and Sheriff's departments were busy with road accidents and stranded motorists, and other nearby rescue teams had their hands full with emergencies of their own. Consequently, the Cochise team was on the go almost non-stop. Meals, mostly nuts, cheese, or dried meat and fruits, were taken on the run, and anyone whose eyes would no longer stay open simply returned to base camp—wherever it happened to be at the time—fell into a sleeping-bag, and slept as long as they had to.

Still, as cold and bone-weary as they were, their spirits rarely sagged: other than the pair of hikers and one of the pilots, who had been killed when his Cessna crashed low on Sulphur Peak, there had been no fatalities. The Cochise team had brought back everyone they had gone after.

And for Jenny, there was another bright note to warm her through the bleak, slogging days and nights. Since she was technically Paul's trainer, they were always members of the same three-person crew, working together, eating together, even grabbing snatches of sleep next to each other in base camp—

and Paul was so busy and so tired that he didn't even make any subtle remarks about 'sleeping together'.

It didn't take her long to discover that the devil-may-care adventurer who was so notoriously careless of his own life never took chances with anyone else's. And although he was a natural leader, and demonstrated it unmistakably more than once, he knew how to follow orders uncomplainingly in the common interest. In no time at all he had become a valuable team player, not merely the 'star' who could easily accomplish climbing feats that no one else would even dare think about. And that was a genuine, highly welcome surprise. As was the closeness and growing trust in each other's abilities that she wouldn't have dreamed possible.

Finally, the frantic activity lessened. The snow melted, the roads returned to normal, the holiday visitors began leaving. Early in the evening of the seventh day, Jenny's crew was recalled to camp. Hank's group had located the two fourteen-year-old boys everyone had been searching for—hungry, cold, and scared, but healthy—and no new calls had come in.

Jenny struggled out of her backpack and with a groan let it fall to the ground at her feet. 'You mean we can actually go home and get some sleep? In a *bed*?' Gratefully, she accepted the mug of coffee Jake handed her. 'And take a *shower*,' she murmured blissfully, 'and put on some clean clothes.'

'And take a shave,' she heard Paul mutter, rubbing his hand over a bristly jaw as he accepted his own mug of coffee.

'Yeah, we sure look like a bunch of bums,' Jake drawled happily. His eyes, lit with pride, travelled over the worn-out team, most of whom leaned against trees, or sat, or lay like so many heaps of dirty laundry among the jumbled backpacks and equipment.

Jake cleared his throat. 'Nice work, folks. We've all earned some rest. Let's go home.'

Jenny only vaguely remembered climbing into the van and sitting next to Paul, then working hard but unsuccessfully to keep her gritty eyelids open. Once, when her head dropped forward with fatigue, she almost slid from her seat, and then she had an even more vague memory of a strong arm encircling her shoulders and pulling her firmly against a broad, comfortable chest. She snuggled in with a sigh, settling her head against the nylon jacket that smelled of wood smoke, and let herself drift contentedly off to sleep on a warm, snug shoulder.

A marvellously comfortable shoulder.

CHAPTER SEVEN

FOR SEVERAL long moments Jenny lay there, her eyes closed, willing herself not to wake up, reluctant to let go of the lovely dream. How marvellous to feel him clasp her to him, and to give herself eagerly up to the power of his mouth, his hands, his long, firm, pressing body, in a way she never could, except in the gauzy, transitory world of dreams.

She dreamed about him often, but this had been the most sensual, realistic one yet. If she lay perfectly quiet, it was almost as if she could still feel the lovely weight of his head on her breasts, and his arm around her waist, and his leg thrown so comfortably over hers.

But sleep was receding; she was awake, or nearly so, and there was the real world to deal with. Regretfully, she stirred—or tried to. Something *was* lying against her breast. She was instantly wide awake. Her eyes flew open to find Paul, deeply asleep, indeed using her for a pillow. How in the world had this happened? *What* had happened? And where was she?

She moved her head carefully to look around. Clearly, they were in the living-room of her apartment. He had moved the rattan chair and pushed the coffee table back so he could spread their open sleeping-bags out on the rug in front of the sofa.

Now, why had he done that? she wondered, a little irritably. He had obviously carried her in from the van while she was still asleep—the last thing she remembered was falling asleep on his shoulder. Well, why had he dumped her on the floor? If he was going to carry her anyway, why hadn't he taken her into her bedroom, and put her on her bed, and——

No, scratch that. This was just fine.

From any standpoint, what he had done was a lot more sensible. She'd been dead to the world, and he couldn't have been in much better shape himself. With them both too tired to bathe and change, this had been the thing to do. He had removed their jackets—shoes too, she found, when she wiggled her toes—and flopped down alongside her. Thank God he hadn't tried to drive on to the ranch. He would have fallen asleep behind the wheel.

She lifted her head a little and looked at him. She could see most of his face. His cheek was against her breast, his arm draped over her ribs. His open hand lay on the blue flannel of the sleeping-bag, relaxed and powerful. She took advantage of the opportunity to study his face, something she couldn't do when he was awake; not when those piercing eyes could turn on her in a fraction of a second and read her thoughts as if they were written on her face in big block letters.

Jenny smiled wryly to herself. Why couldn't he look the way other people did when they were sleeping? Why didn't he look vacant, or weak, or puffy-faced? Why didn't he snore, or at least make repulsive bubbling sounds when he breathed? But no, just as she might have predicted, his face lost none of its strength or quiet self-confidence in sleep, and he breathed quietly and regularly, his mouth closed, as attractive as ever, even with matted hair and a week's growth of wiry beard. Damn the man, he didn't fight fair!

The top two or three buttons of his shirt had come open, and she could see the dark mat of hair on the broad, slablike muscles of his chest. Her hand was lying inches away. How pleasant it would be to move her arm so that her hand lay flat against the warm centre of his chest, her fingers twined lightly in the curls. He would never even know it, and——

She blushed abruptly and let her head fall back. What was she coming to? Taking advantage of a helpless, sleeping man! She almost laughed aloud, but, really, it wasn't funny. There was no denying the way she felt at this moment, with their bodies so intimately—yet innocently—wound together. What she felt was hunger, a hunger as insistent as the need for food. She was hungry for him in the deepest part of her; there was nothing more she wanted from the world than to be allowed to stay pressed against him, just like this, for ever.

For ever? My God, she thought with a sinking, dizzy sense of dismay, she'd gone and done it: she had fallen in love with him despite everything she'd been telling herself. More likely, she had loved him since the first time she had seen him, lying under the wreckage on that cold, starlit night, high in the Chirieahuas, and only now was she ready to admit it to herself. Either way, she thought desolately, fighting a sudden, panicky urge to weep, she was in for nothing but pain.

With the world his oyster, if Paul had been the marrying kind he would have been snapped up years ago. But he wasn't the marrying kind, and even if he were, the thought that he would ever think about spending his life with the ordinary, provincial Jenny Roberts—providing she could bring herself to cope with his hare-brained approach to life—was laughable.

Well, anyway, after this last week, there was the comforting thought that they were at least on the way to being good friends. Somehow, though, there wasn't much solace in it. Maybe good friends shouldn't lie around on each other like this.

'Paul . . .' She shook his shoulder. 'Paul, wake up.'

He stirred without opening his eyes, and her breath caught in her throat as he resettled his cheek against her breast and pulled his arm tighter around her waist.

Even asleep he made things hard for her!

She shook him harder, trying unsuccessfully to struggle out from under him into a sitting position.

'Mmm, don't move,' he murmured sleepily, his eyes still closed. 'Nice.' His face moved maddeningly against her breast and settled in again. Around her waist his arm was like a steel band.

'Paul, let me up,' she pleaded. 'This is embarrassing. It's almost eight-thirty in the morning. What if somebody comes by? What will they think?'

He sighed petulantly, finally coming awake, although his eyes stayed closed—and his cheek remained right where it was. 'They'll think we spent

the night sleeping together. Which is true enough,'
he added with a lazy, closed-eyed grin. Then, after
another sigh, his eyes reluctantly opened. There
could be no question now but that he was quite aware
of exactly where his face was, but he showed no
inclination to move.

'Paul!'

Regretfully, he moved at last, straightening up
enough to prop his chin on his hand. He lifted his
eyes to her face for the first time. And winced. 'Good
lord, is this what you always look like in the
morning?'

As usual, he'd managed to ignite her temper with
almost his first sentence.

'When I've been out in the field for seven days,
yes!' she snapped. Not that she was exactly at her best
when she first woke up in any case. She was a wriggly
sleeper who generally woke up a tangled-haired
mess. Nothing like those 'simpering sex-kittens' he
was used to, she was certain. She could imagine what
she must look like now; it was awful to have him
assessing her so coolly. 'And you're not exactly
looking like Robert Redford yourself!' she added
angrily. Maybe not, she told herself in a rueful aside,
but good enough. Not that she would tell him so.

He grinned and rubbed his shadowed jaw. It made
a sound like sandpaper. 'You're probably right,' he
said good-naturedly. 'I must look terrible. Maybe
even as bad as you do.'

'Thanks a lot,' she grumbled as she struggled up.

Rolling over on his back, he settled a pillow under
his head and watched her comfortably. 'You mad

about something?' he asked pleasantly.

'Mad?' Her tone was sardonic. 'Me?'

'Well, that's a relief,' he smiled, looking very much at his ease lying there, as if it were his apartment, not hers. 'So, how do we decide who gets first crack at the shower?'

'Easy!' Jenny yelled, and ran for the bathroom door.

Even with the advantage of surprise, she barely got it closed and locked before his hand was on the knob.

'Highly unsportsmanlike,' she heard him mutter with acid amusement. 'It's not *my* fault the woman looks like a wreck.'

When she looked in the mirror she winced no less painfuly than he had on seeing her. Paul had been politely restrained in merely calling her a wreck. Well, at least it was all repairable. She searched in the top drawer of the cabinet for her manicure scissors. Her hair was so snarled from having slept with a rubber band in it, she'd have to cut the thing out. That job accomplished (and a few locks of hair gone with it), she turned the shower on full blast and spent a few blissful minutes simply standing under it and savouring the steaming, hot water before soaping down and shampooing her hair.

When she was done, she slipped into her bedroom and called out to Paul that the shower was all his. Quickly, she blow-dried her hair until it fell in soft, wonderfully clean waves on her shoulders, and put the merest touch of make-up on lips and cheeks. It was wonderful to step into a pair of crisp, white jeans

and a teal-blue, raglan-sleeve sweater that was as soft
as swandsdown against her skin. She sighed with
pleasure. How nice it was to feel human once more,
to be *clean*, to be out of the filthy clothes she'd worn
for so long! She smiled at herself in the mirror,
pleased with the way the blue of the sweater
deepened the colour of her eyes. It was nice to look
like a woman again, too.

Her exterior restored, she went out to the kitchen
to give some attention to her stomach, which had
been clamouring unnoticed for some time. She was
morosely contemplating the week-old food in the
refrigerator, when Paul came up behind her.

He, too, looked refreshed. Apparently, he'd had
the foresight to put a change of clothes in his car
because he was dressed in a bulky brown sweater and
tan trousers. He'd brought a razor too, but,
obviously, he had still been half-asleep when he'd
shaved; there was a tiny adhesive plaster on his jaw-
line. Jenny had to fight the sympathetic impulse to
reach up and touch his cheek.

'You know,' he said, his green eyes travelling
appreciatively over her, 'if you'd looked like that an
hour ago, you'd never have made it out of the living-
room, no matter *how* fast you'd run.' His voice
dropped lower, to a near-whisper. 'You wouldn't
have made it off the floor.'

He had said it with a husky edge to his voice, and
now he moved closer, hand raised, fingertips gently
running over the outline over her cheek and then
brushing back the hair at her temple. 'Interested in
trying a re-run?'

Jenny gulped. Her legs had turned to butter with his words, and her spine was in just about the same condition. How could that warm camaraderie they had developed over the week so quickly change into this dangerous by-play? *She* might envision a possible future of good friendship between them, but Paul clearly had other ideas.

'The only thing I'm interested in is food,' she replied with all the nonchalance she could muster, which wasn't much, 'and I'm afraid we'll have to go shopping for it.'

'Or go out,' he replied, and his hand left her face. 'The Copper King does a terrific steak and eggs breakfast.'

'You're on,' Jenny answered, swinging the refrigerator door shut. The sooner they were out of her apartment, with other people around, the better.

His eloquent eyebrows rose. '"You're on" . . . just like that? No argument about how you can't possibly have breakfast with me? How even though the bank's closed on Saturdays you have to go to work?'

'Pass up steak and eggs for mouldy cheese and stale bread, or a trip to the store? No way!' she joked. 'Right this minute, I'd eat with the devil himself for a square meal.' She smiled. 'No personal reference intended, of course.'

His broad mouth quirked at the edges. 'Then after we eat I have a good idea for what we can do for some well-earned fun.'

She hesitated. 'What?'

'Food first.' He caught her hand, lacing his fingers through hers, and pulled her through the living-room. 'Then we'll talk plans.'

Jenny hadn't the will to argue and there was no point in being coy. No point in arguing with him either, when it came to that. She knew she wanted to be with him, and it wasn't hard to see that he knew it, too. Not that steak and eggs at the Copper King *didn't* sound sublime.

They were half-way out of the door when Jenny remembered.

'It's Saturday, the twenty-second!' she exclaimed, with a groan of disappointment. 'The avalanche seminar! We should have flown out *yesterday*!'

Paul was caught by surprise, too. 'The twenty-second? Already? Damn!' He frowned. 'Well, it's no wonder it slipped our minds.' He looked at his watch, quickly calculating. 'We can make most of it, anyway. It's too late for this morning's session, but we can be there in time for this afternoon's—even with a breakfast stop ... and I'm not flying anywhere until I get some hot food in me. We'll leave from the Copper King, so go throw some clothes in an overnight bag.'

While Jenny hurriedly complied in the bedroom, Paul shouted an afterthought from the living-room. 'And put in something decent to wear in case we get a chance to go out for dinner. There's a lodge just a few miles away.'

Fortunately there was no wait for a table at the Copper King. After a week of camp fare, the food tasted glorious, and they were so hungry that conversation was suspended until they had demolished their steaks, eggs, and country-fried potatoes.

Finally, Paul leaned back, lathered boysenberry jam thickly on to the last of his sourdough biscuits, and nodded at the waiter to refill their coffees.

'I don't know when I enjoyed a meal more than that,' he said with a convincingly contented sigh.

'Or spent a more virtuous week?' Jenny teased, also leaning comfortably back.

'Virtuous? Me? I was just too tired to be anything else.'

'That isn't what I meant. I meant that you just spent seven days being productive and useful—saving people's lives. And,' she added, 'you did it very well.'

His brows knitted in mock concern. 'Why, you're right! I hadn't looked at it that way. Good lord, if this gets out my reputation will be absolutely ruined. What will people think?'

'I imagine your secret's safe,' she said, laughing. 'It won't make the *New York Times*, and I doubt if many of your friends subscribe to the *Cochise Bend Observer*.' She set down her coffee cup. 'Well, that ought to last me until dinner.'

'Lunch, anyway,' Paul rejoined, picking up the bill. 'You sure can pack it away.'

'Well, I get a lot of exercise——' Jenny began stiffly.

Laughing, he held up his hand like a traffic policeman. 'Simmer down, Jenny. I was admiring you, not insulting you. It's a great change to eat a meal with a woman who's not on some five-hundred-calorie-a-day diet of cottage cheese and turnips, that's all.' His eyes drifted over her in a distinctly proprietorial way that should have put her teeth on edge but most certainly did not. 'Whatever kind of diet you're on,' he said spiritedly, 'I hope you stay on it!'

Jenny seemed to float out of the restaurant on a cloud, but she came back down to earth when they stopped at the Lathan ranch so Paul could pick up some clothes and check on the ranch hands. A message from Peter MacCabe was waiting on the blue notepad by the telephone.

Paul read it, his teeth sunk in his lower lip. 'The seminar's been cancelled,' he said. 'Sounds like Peter was as busy as we were during the storm, and he just couldn't prepare for it.' He tossed the note back on the counter. 'Don't look so disappointed. Nothing's stopping us from taking a trip, anyway. In fact, that's what I was going to suggest before—that we spend the weekend at Yosemite. Ever been there in the spring? The falls are at their best.'

It was true that she'd been disappointed for a moment, but now an avid excitement leaped inside her.

'Well ... actually, I've never been there at all, but——'

'We could do some skiing. There are some nice runs in the high country, up at Badger Pass. And don't tell me that you don't know how to ski.'

Skiing in southern Arizona wasn't easy to do, but of course that wouldn't occur to a man like Paul, who could fly six hundred miles on a whim. 'Well, I don't——' she said defensively.

'No problem; I'll teach you. And don't tell me that

you don't have the right things to wear.'

'But I don't. How would I——?'

'And don't tell me that you can't afford it.'

'Will you stop telling me what I can't tell you?' she asked, laughing in spite of herself. 'Anyway, I can't! And if——'

He continued serenely, 'Because I'm inviting you, so naturally I'm paying for everything. And as I may have told you once or twice, I don't——'

'——take no for an answer. I know.'

'Fine,' he said, zipping up a soft leather shoulder-bag, 'everything's settled.'

'Well . . . all right, but we're going to have to come to an understanding about some things——'

'Sure, fine. We can do it on the way.' He grinned at her and slung the bag over his shoulder. 'OK, let's go . . . and no more arguments. Just do as you're told, for a change.

'Mr Brant,' she said briskly, 'has anyone ever told you that you embody all the characteristics of the worst kind of male chauvinist?'

'Yes, you,' Paul laughed, with a shrug of his wide shoulders, 'but as long as you keep complimenting me, why should I complain?'

'Why, Mr Brant!' the desk manager exclaimed with a broad smile. 'Well, well, well, it's a pleasure to see you again!' He made a clucking noise with his tongue and lowered his voice to a gossipy whisper. 'I read about your crash in New Mexico——'

'Arizona,' Paul said.

'Yes, of course; Arizona. In the Choctaws——'

'Chiricahuas.'

'Ah,' the man said, 'yes. Quite so. Well, I'm happy to see you in good health, sir.'

'Thank you, Raymond,' Paul said. 'Think you can find a couple of rooms for us?' Raymond laughed at the absurdity of the question. 'For *you*, Mr Brant? Of course. The Tuolomne Lodge is always honoured to have you as a guest.'

Paul looked at Jenny and winked. On the flight she had shown her surprise when he told her he hadn't bothered to call ahead for reservations at Yosemite Valley's grand old inn. 'Isn't that place always booked?' she had asked. 'You can't just walk in and get a room, can you?' But he'd only shrugged and said, 'We'll just try our luck and see how it goes.'

'Try our luck', indeed! Jenny was getting a very heady taste of what it was like to be rich and famous. She wondered wryly what sort of reception she would have got from Raymond had she shown up all by herself without a reservation.

'Let's see, now . . .' Raymond said, examining his ledger. Jenny felt a slight surge of guilt. Some poor, ordinary mortal who had dutifully made his reservation months before was about to be shifted to less desirable quarters.

'Ah.' Raymond picked up his pen, then looked up at Paul with a mildly puzzled frown. 'You, ah, did say you wanted *two* rooms for yourself and the young lady?'

'Certainly,' said Paul blandly. 'What else?'

Raymond cleared his throat discreetly. 'Very good, sir. I have just the thing: two adjoining suites with marvellous views of Half-Dome.'

'One of those will be fine for me,' Paul said suavely, 'but Miss Roberts is on a budget.' Keeping a straight face, although Jenny knew well enough that he found the situation comic—and novel as well, obviously—he suggested, 'Maybe one of those old attic rooms with the bathroom down the hall?'

He was overdoing it a little, but Jenny really couldn't complain. This was all part of the 'understanding' she had insisted on. Paul's basic plan had been far too atttractive to turn down, but she had agreed to go only if he would let her pay for her own lodging—separate lodging, she had made clear. And she'd got his promise that if he wanted to go skiing he would go alone. She had no wish to experience the pleasures of an expensive hobby she couldn't afford.

'An attic room would be fine.' Jenny addressed Raymond, tilting her chin upward. 'And as for views, the back car park will do very well. I can go outside when I want to look at Half-Dome.'

Raymond, trying unsuccessfully to hide his curiosity, turned again to the register with a look that expressed pain at the idea that the Tuolomne Lodge might have such rooms. 'I think,' he said fussily, 'that we can do a bit better than that for a friend of Mr Brant's. And,' he hastily assured her, 'at a most economical rate.' He removed two keys from the board behind him and gestured to two waiting bellboys.

With a wave and a casual 'Meet you back here in half an hour,' Paul followed one of the bellboys through the enormous pannelled lobby with its hanging American Indian rugs, past the massive fireplace of rustic stone, and up the broad wooden stairs. And Jenny was whisked down a narrow, inconspicuous corridor to the right of the reception desk.

But despite the unpromising plainness of the hall that led to it, Jenny was pleased and surprised by her tiny corner room with its cheerful red and yellow plaid curtains and matching bedspread. It was like a little girl's room; bright, and fresh, and clean. The view through the multi-paned windows did actually include a small corner of the back car park, but most of it was a fairyland-like landscape of snow-laden pine forest and meadow, noisy with the jaunty chattering of birds and chipmunks. By leaning out of the open window, she discovered she could, after all, see much of Half-Dome's awesome, vertical, granite face at the eastern end of the valley. No wonder people went on so endlessly about Yosemite. She'd seen photographs of it, of course, but still, she'd had no idea . . .

It was one thing to look at pretty pictures, or to read about a great, green valley that is seven miles long, a mile wide, and three thousand feet deep, with towering granite cliffs and domes, and waterfalls plunging all the way from the rim to the forested valley floor. It was another thing entirely to see it. And to *feel* it—because Yosemite Falls' stupendous flood of water produced a shuddering thunder that could be felt anywhere in the valley. No one had ever told her about that, and she still could hardly believe it.

And for the first time she really understood why this area, although it had no huge mountains— nothing like Rainier or Whitney, or a hundred others—presented the greatest rock-climbing challenges in North America ... for the select group of climbers who knew how, and were crazy enough, to pull themselves up smooth, perpendicular rock-faces that soared thousands of feet without anything that a sensible climber might think of as a handhold.

Idly wondering if Paul had ever climbed here, she pulled her head back in and closed the window. Suddenly she laughed, feeling unreasonably happy, and even twirled briefly in the centre of the room. Why shouldn't she be happy, really? She had a whole, lovely day and a half here in this glorious place, and when she left it would be on another spectacular aeroplane flight—never again would she be content with a six-mile-high seat in a commercial jet after having skimmed over the rivers and forests at 4,000 feet, right in the cockpit! It was almost too much to be believed.

True, she'd have to keep her guard up, but she would manage—after all, she'd won the little skirmish over separate rooms and separate bills with ease, and she hadn't even made him angry in doing it.

Unzipping her overnight bag, she pulled out a simple tan sweater, jeans, and hiking boots. Not quite as homely as her Huckleberry Finn outfit, but certainly nothing that would give him the idea that she was trying to encourage his attentions. Not that she had anything to match the Norwegian and

Scottish sweaters, or the satiny, body-hugging ski-wear that the svelte women lounging about the lobby had been wearing. Where did all those elegant females come from, anyway? she thought irritatedly. You sure never saw them around Cochise Bend!

When she came into the lobby she saw Paul at once, in a secluded corner, leaning close to one of those inhumanly attractive women, his head thrown back in intimate, confident laughter. It certainly hadn't taken him long to run into one of his sex kittens, she thought resentfully. Her vision blurred with the unexpected shock of a raw, slicing stab of jealousy that squeezed her heart like a cold, iron fist.

She caught herself just before she turned on the spot and marched bitterly back to her room. What in the world was she thinking of? How could she be jealous of a man whose romantic interests she was trying to discourage? Oh, dear! This battle with her own emotions grew harder and more bewildering all the time. Well, she wasn't going to run off and hide just because Paul had come upon an old flame. Or even a current one. She squared her shoulders and walked up to them.

'Ah, Jenny,' Paul said, still laughing at whatever had passed between them. 'I was wondering what happened to you.'

Oh, sure, Jenny thought sourly. I could see how worried you were.

'Jenny Roberts,' he said formally, 'Cynthia van Leyden.'

Even her name was fancy. Jenny fixed a smile on

her face, murmured something, and examined the
tall, slender woman with the glorious red-gold hair
straight out of a shampoo commercial. High, smooth
forehead; lithe, feline body encased in a sky-blue ski
outfit that fitted like a pelt; confident, casual
elegance that was the female counterpart of Paul's
masculine grace. Jenny hated her on sight.
Passionately.

Cynthia van Leyden smiled. 'Paul's told me a little
about you,' she said with unanticipated friendliness.
'It sounds as if you actually got him to do something
useful last week. And they said it couldn't be done.'
She laughed and held out her hand. 'I'm really glad
to know you,' she said with transparent warmth.

This was terrible! Cynthia van Leyden was *nice*!
Jenny couldn't even hate Paul's women friends with
an easy conscience!

She smiled back at Cynthia—a genuine smile this
time. 'I'm glad to know you, too.' She gestured at the
blue outfit. 'Have you been out on the slopes?'

'All day.' Then, eagerly, 'Do you ski, Jenny?'

'No, I'm afraid not.'

'And she won't let me teach her,' Paul drawled, a
touch of exasperation in his voice. He glanced at
Jenny, one eyebrow raised. 'We have an
"understanding".'

'I don't blame her.' Cynthia laughed. 'Would you
even recognise a beginner's slope if you saw one?'
She turned to Jenny. 'I'd be happy to give you a
couple of lessons to get you started if you'd like. I've
taught my kid brothers, and I know how scary it
seems at first.'

'That's awfully kind of you,' Jenny said, 'but I don't think it's my kind of sport.' Not financially, anyway, she amended in regretful silence, because except for that little aspect she couldn't think of another sport that appealed to her more.

'Well, let me know if you change your mind,' Cynthia said, and seemed to mean it. 'I've got to run now.' She smiled at Jenny, then squeezed Paul's arm. 'I'm supposed to meet Sandy outside——'

'Sandy?' Paul said with interest. 'Is Sandy here, too?'

'Yes, we're off to the Badger Pass run.'

'Right,' Paul said. 'Well, say hi for me. And have fun.' He kissed her on the cheek. 'See you both later.'

'She seems very nice,' Jenny said, through lips that felt as if they were carved from wood.

'She *is* very nice,' Paul said, still looking fondly after her. 'All right,' he said at last, when Cynthia had disappeared gracefully through the door, 'what would you like to do?'

'Paul, you don't have to worry about me,' she said. 'If you want to go join your ski-bunny friends up on the slopes, go ahead.'

He blinked with surprise. 'Ski-bunny?'

'Oh, maybe not,' she muttered, staring at the floor. She was ashamed of herself. Cynthia van Leyden had been as ladylike and pleasant to her as anyone could be, and here she was, taking potshots at her behind her back. 'Look,' she said sullenly, 'all I meant was that I can amuse myself perfectly well, so go ahead and go skiing if that's what you want to do.'

Paul laughed. 'Well, what are *you* mad about?'

How could she tell him, when she hardly understood herself? She was angry because the beautiful Cyhthia van Leyden had appeared out of nowhere to spoil the weekend, and that she was gracious and kind. But would she have been less angry had Cynthia snubbed her? And she was angry at the restrained way Paul had kissed her high-boned, tawny cheek, as if he were going out of his way to be decorous for *her* benefit. But would she have liked it better had he taken Cynthia in his arms and kissed her on that smooth, glossy mouth? And mostly she was angry at what a clear, unmistakable gulf yawned between her own narrow world and the easy, confident world of the beautiful people that Cynthia and Paul inhabited so casually. Still, hadn't she been trying to make him see that gulf since she'd met him?

None of it made sense, but then what had, since he'd literally fallen into her life from out of the sky? Oh, well, at least she hadn't been bored.

He grasped her chin and made her look up at him. 'Come on, now, what's bothering you?'

As always, that heartbreakingly clear gaze, as cool and clean as the glacier-fed water that ran through the valley, drove everything from her mind; everything but him. And suddenly she wasn't angry any more; she was glad. Glad to have him standing next to her, touching her, glad to be in Yosemite, glad to be alive.

'Nothing's bothering me—really.'

He looked doubtful. 'Would you like to have a

drink in the lounge?' he asked. 'Stu makes a hell of a whisky toddy.'

She shook her head. 'Could we go outside?'

'Sure. How about a ride around the valley on the shuttle?' He pointed to the double-decker sightseeing bus pulling up in front of the lodge. Mostly it was full of skiers who were riding it to one of the transfer points for other shuttles up to the ski lifts, but a few hardy, bundled-up sightseers sat on the roofless upper level.

'I'd love it!' she said enthusiastically. 'But I want to sit on top, in the open, so I can see everything!'

Despite the fact that they had driven from the Merced airport to the park in a rental car, the last seven miles through the valley had been more frustrating than anything else. Even by craning her neck, Jenny hadn't been able to see the cliff tops from the car window because of the narrowness of the valley.

'We'll freeze,' Paul said, 'but all right. Run and get a jacket. I'll get the driver to wait.'

The front seats on the top deck were empty, just as she had hoped, and Jenny sat down contentedly, nestling against Paul without quite snuggling up to him. The bus immediately glided on its way, generating an icy draft that would have chilled her at any other time, but somehow felt delightfully fresh and bracing now.

They didn't talk for some minutes. Jenny sat as close to him as she could get, her head up, her eyes moving from side to side, drinking in the white-etched canyon walls, the snow-laden pines high above, sparkling in the golden afternoon sunlight, the long, threadlike streams of water that were everywhere, wafting down half a mile and more, with dreamlike slowness, from the icy white valley rim to the lush and almost snow-free bottom.

'So many waterfalls,' she murmured. 'They're everywhere. I didn't know.'

'Most people don't. They only flow in March and April. Frozen before, dry afterwards, except for the biggest.'

'Mm,' Jenny said, still hungrily gazing about her.

She shivered, perhaps with cold, perhaps with pleasure, perhaps with something else. Who knew any more?

'Chilly?' Paul asked.

She was about to say no, but she realised that he would put his arm around her if she said she were. 'Mm—hm,' she said. 'Very.'

And he did put his arm around her shoulders and pull her even a little closer to him. 'Better?'

'Mm,' she said, floating off into her own private paradise. If things could just stay like this for ever, without changes or complications: just the cold, fresh air, the majestic waterfalls, the closeness of Paul, his warm, protective strength ... She sighed lazily, burrowing into him. Wasn't it only this morning she'd awakened in a far more intimate embrace, wishing *that* could go on for ever? That had been lovely too, especially following as it had on that dream of passion and abandon ...

'Penny,' he said.

'Hmm?' she murmured sleepily.

'For your thoughts. You were smiling. What were you thinking about?'

'Oh, I was just thinking how wonderful——' She started, then straightened up in her seat, her mind alert just in time. She improvised hurriedly. '——how wonderful it is here,' she finished lamely.

She glanced timidly at him, wondering how much he'd been able to read in that unconscious smile.

Apparently, he had read it like a neon sign, because he was grinning at her, his eyes flickering amusedly over her face. His arm still lay casually over the back of her seat. 'Oh, is that what you were thinking?'

'Yes, of course' she said primly. 'What did you suppose?'

His grin widened. 'Me? Not a thing.'

The bus came to one of its stops, and six or eight skiers got off. One of them, every bit as beautiful as Cynthia van Leyden, but with raven hair and smooth, ivory skin, looked boldly up at Paul, somehow sensing his presence. She smiled at him with an invitation in her dark eyes that was so open Jenny was embarrassed. Paul smiled back, and the bus moved off, leaving the woman gazing hotly after him.

'Another old friend?' Jenny asked.

'Nope.'

'Oh? Is that the way strange women always react to you?'

'Yup. Well,' he added modestly, 'maybe not *always*.'

'That must be nice for you,' Jenny said coolly. Her

lovely day was deteriorating rapidly.

'Not that nice,' he said curtly.

Surprised, she turned to look at him. He was staring straight ahead, his expression unreadable, his eyes on the pyramidal spires of the Three Sisters, now coming into view around a bend to the left.

'Tell me,' he said expressionlessly. 'What did you think of Cynthia?'

Jenny's heart thudded. 'I . . . liked her,' she said carefully, not sure where he was leading.

'Really? Even though she's a "ski-bunny"?'

Jenny blushed, but was annoyed, too. She didn't like being reminded that a great deal of the time these days she wasn't at her best. 'I suppose she's a good skier,' she said, trying to be gracious. But she didn't feel gracious.

'A good skier?' Paul responded with a laugh. 'If you followed skiing, you'd have recognised her name. She took a second in the women's downhill at the World Cup in Grenoble last year. Pretty nice of her to offer to teach you, I'd say.'

'Very,' Jenny agreed huskily, ashamed of her jaundiced reaction to a woman who had gone out of her way to be nice, but at the same time wishing with all her heart that Cynthia were still in Grenoble, or even farther away. 'Have you known her long?'

Paul's eyes gleamed with mischief, but she had dropped hers to stare fixedly at the railing in front of her and she didn't notice. 'Oh, for three or four years now,' he said. 'She's a terrific person. We usually run into each other quite a lot during the ski season:

Kitzbühel, Sun Valley, Garmisch, Innsbruck . . . you know.'

No, Jenny did not know. She stared mutely at the railing, picking with a gloved finger at the chipped paint.

If Paul were aware that she was sulking, he didn't show it. 'She's really something, isn't she?' he went on airily. 'Beautiful, great athlete, lots of fun . . . intelligent . . .'

'Modest too, no doubt,' Jenny offered bleakly, afraid he might have been about to rave to her about the superlative Cynthia's abilities in bed.

Paul considered, then nodded. 'That too,' he said judiciously. 'I hadn't thought about that.'

His hand lying just behind her shoulders moved forward, lightly stroking her cheek, playing with a lock of hair loosened by the wind. 'I don't know why,' he said, 'but I get the impression that you're mad again. What happened?' She could hear the grin in his voice without looking at him. 'Get up on the wrong side of the bed this morning?'

She jerked her head irritably away from his fingers and forced herself to speak. 'And I don't know why,' she said crisply, 'you keep thinking I'm angry. I'm not.'

'Ah.'

'I'm just . . . Well, since she's so perfect, I can't help wondering why you haven't snapped her up a long time ago.'

'You know, I just might have done that,' he replied, 'but of course that would have upset Sandy.'

'Sandy . . .? Oh, the friend she's skiing with. No,'

Jenny said bitterly, 'you certainly wouldn't want to upset her.' She wished she knew the valley terrain, so that she could get out and walk back to the lodge.

'You better believe I wouldn't. Sandy's six-foot-six and two hundred and forty pounds.'

Jenny stared open-mouthed at him.

'Sandy's a "he",' he explained quietly. 'And he's not Cynthia's friend, he's her husband.' His eyes, filled with charm and tender amusement, locked with hers. 'Now, what do you think of that?' he asked softly.

It was as if a strap slowly squeezing her heart had snapped. She took a full, deep breath for the first time in some minutes. 'You . . . you rat!' she exclaimed, as indignant as she was relieved. 'You've been leading me on!'

'Leading you on?' He laughed. Well, maybe, just a little.'

'A *little*?' She lifted her clenched fists, not at all sure what she was going to do with them, but he caught both wrists easily, still laughing, and lowered them to her lap.

'I was just proving a point—to both of us.'

'What point?' She sat very still.

'That you're jealous of me. And that,' he said, shifting to let go of her wrists and take hold of her hands, 'is a very good sign indeed.'

'I don't think it's a good sign at all,' Jenny said as they started off again. 'It's a bad sign, a *terrible* sign——'

The bus slowed to a stop at Curry Village, and on sudden impulse she pulled her hands from his, dashed down the metal steps and out of the bus, and broke into a run, to the amazement of passengers and bus driver.

To Paul's amazement, too. She was half-way down the stairs before he reacted, and twenty feet down the road before he caught up with her.

'Jenny——'

Blindly she tried to pull herself out of his grasp, but he gathered her in, pressing her to him with something like desperation.

For once the sweet, inexorable power of his body didn't work its magic. She sobbed and turned her head away, twisting her face in his hands.

'Jenny, what is it?' he said, his face tense with concern.

'Oh, Paul, Paul,' she cried through her tears, 'don't you see? This is just a game to you, an ego trip, but for me ——'

'Ego trip?' He stared incredulously at her. 'Is that all you think it is?'

'All right, maybe more,' she said, dabbing at her eyes, conscious of the busful of rapt, wide-eyed people being dragged reluctantly away. 'I'll admit there's some physical attraction involved——'

'That's big of you,' he said, the smile beginning to return.

'——but I'm—I'm not as used to this kind of thing as you are. I can't just—just have an affair with a man and forget it—the way you can . . .'

'I think,' he said drily, 'that I'd have an even harder time than you, forgetting an affair with a man.'

She smiled weakly, in spite of herself.

'That's better.' He handed her a pristine handker-chief. 'Now dry your eyes and let's walk.'

She obeyed him wordlessly, and after they had walked for a few minutes, he said, 'Can you really think you just represent an ego trip and a casual affair to me?'

Jenny hardly knew what she thought. She continued walking, waiting for him to continue.

'If that's all it was, why do you think I've been spending all this time—these weeks—spending all this time . . .'

It always shocked her to see him at a loss for words. 'Spending all this time what?' she asked, genuinely curious.

'Well . . . courting you,' he ground out, hands in his pockets, head scrunched down, like a ten-year-old boy forced to admit that maybe girls were all right, after all.

'*Courting* me?' Jenny stopped, frozen with astonishment.

'Well, you don't have to shout it,' he said sheepishly, looking around him, as if he was embarrassed that someone might hear. No doubt he was. He took her by the arm and started her walking again.

She moved on unresistingly, in a daze. 'C-courting me?' she said again, stammering in her confusion. 'Do you mean you want . . . that you . . .' The words dried up. No, it was impossible.

'That I love you?' Paul said, not looking at her. 'That I want to marry you? Is that what you mean?'

She was afraid to say anything at all. This was

another dream. If she spoke it would end. She nodded her head dumbly. They had stopped walking again, and stood looking at each other under a long, sun-dappled canopy of firs and pines.

Paul turned to her, looking at her very hard, in a way he had never looked at her before. 'The answer to your first question's "yes",' he said, and the lucid, penetrating green gaze softened. So did his voice. 'And the answer to the second one is also "yes".'

Jenny looked at him, her eyes wide with wonder. 'I ... I can hardly believe we're having this conversation.'

'Why not?' His face relaxed suddenly. The old, amused, self-confident smile was back. 'Look, if all I'd wanted was to get you into bed, believe me, I know faster ways to go about it than whatever it is I've been trying to do.' He shrugged. 'Which is to get your approval, I guess.'

'Is that what you've been doing?' Jenny was still trying to decide if this were really happening.

He laughed. 'Of all the women in the world who would jump at the chance to marry me for all the important things—I'm rich, I'm generous, I'm a hunk—I have to fall in love with someone who's all hung up on trivialities like character, for God's sake.'

Jenny laughed. 'But I never believed ... it never occurred to me you could be doing anything but having a fling.'

'Even when I couldn't help worrying about you all the time? Blowing up when I found out you'd walked home alone that first night?'

'Well, I must admit it seemed pretty strange,

coming from you.'

They began walking again, slowly and thoughtfully. 'It was strange, all right,' he said. 'I'm not the
protective type. I've never felt anything like that
about a woman before. And that's despite the fact
that you're one of the most competent people I've
ever met.'

Jenny glowed, beginning to believe she might not
wake up from this after all. 'Truly?'

'Truly.' He reached for her hand and held it as
they walked. 'Jenny, I haven't been the same since I
heard your voice coming out of the blackness, telling
me to hang on. Do you know, you've given me a
reason to live . . . a reason to look at my life and see
what a meaningless mess I was making out of it.' He
glanced sideways at her with a smile that was almost
shy. 'I need you, Jenny. In every way a man needs a
woman.'

They stopped again, on the quiet path, in the
growing dusk, and looked into each other's eyes.
Jenny thought her heart might burst from joy. Paul
put his hands on either side of her face and guided
her mouth with gentle firmness to his. They kissed in
a way they never had before, almost chastely, their
lips brushing. He kissed her chin, her cheeks, her
lowered eyelids, her forehead, all as softly and
carefully—and respectfully—as if she were a fragile,
priceless porcelain sculpture.

CHAPTER EIGHT

JENNY brushed her hair slowly, staring into the mirror without seeing anything, trying to put into perspective what was happening to her. Some time before, she had read an article about people who had won million-dollar lotteries, and she'd been surprised to find out that almost every one of them had wound up more discontented and unhappy in the end than they had been before. Sudden wealth had cut them off from their old friends, and had made it harder, not easier, to make genuine new ones, so that they no longer fitted comfortably anywhere, but wandered like people without countries, trusting no one, fitting nowhere.

Well, having a Paul Brant tumble to the earth like a gift from the gods, fall in love with her and want to marry her was a lot like winning a lottery. And with about the same odds, she reflected; about two million to one. She'd never dreamed such a thing could happen, and if she had, she'd have had the good sense not to wish for it. But it was one thing not to wish for something, and another to turn it down when it was offered for the taking. He actually *loved* her. It was simply too fantastic! She still couldn't quite take it in.

She put her hairbrush on the dressing-table and stared hard at herself in the mirror. She didn't look like a woman who'd just received a proposal of marriage from the man she loved more than anything

146

in the world. There was a lost, troubled look in her eyes, her skin was flushed, and her mouth wasn't quite steady.

The truth was, Jenny didn't know what she wanted to do. Oh, she didn't have any doubts about how she felt about him, about how desperately she wanted him—and yet the idea of marrying him . . .

She had thoroughly shocked him when she'd asked for time to think about it, and the thought brought a small smile to her lips. It had taken all of five seconds after that lovely, gentle kiss for her to blurt out how much she loved him, and he had taken that—which hadn't surprised him in the least, of course—to mean everything was settled. But when he had begun to talk about honeymoon plans she'd interrupted and told him she wasn't sure about it at all; she wanted an hour or two to herself, and she would give him her answer at dinner.

'Give me your answer. . .!' he'd exclaimed, candidly astonished at the idea that any female might turn him down. For a moment his eyes had blazed angrily, but then he'd treated it as a kind of joke, as if Jenny were merely playing by her own rules, and there wasn't really any question about the outcome. So he would be a good sport and go along with her.

But there was a question, a big question.

'What an idiot I was to fall in love with him!' she moaned to her reflection, wondering how he would react to the condition she was going to ask him to agree to tonight. Without it, she couldn't marry him; she just couldn't.

He was going to have to promise to quit his crazy, reckless approach to life. He was going to have to stop taking risks for risk's sake. Jenny was uncomfortable with the idea of telling someone else how to run his life, but she simply couldn't face the prospect of years of sitting alone, wondering if he had fallen off his twenty-thousand-foot mountain, or gone down in his one-man boat in the middle of the Caspian Sea, or got away from the head hunters chasing him through the jungles of New Guinea.

It wasn't simply faintheartedness on her part. Search-and-rescue work was dangerous too, yet his interest in it was a bright spot in her life. Sure, he might fall off a cliff rescuing someone just as she might, but there would be a reason for his death—a reason for his *life*—that would be there through the agony of losing him. But to risk death for no reason? For the 'fun' of it? She shivered. It was impossible that his fiendishly good luck could continue to last if he kept treating his life as contemptuously as he did, and she didn't want to be there when it ran out.

She turned gloomily away from the mirror and pulled her jumpsuit off the hanger. As bright and pretty as it was, she couldn't help feeling as if she were dressing for a funeral. Paul wasn't the sort of man who let others dictate to him. Was it possible that he would agree to her terms? She doubted it. And if he didn't, would she really have the strength to stick to her guns and turn him down? She doubted that, too. Things didn't look good at all.

She shook her head, wryly conscious of the paradoxical situation she found herself in. Who would have thought that an unhoped-for declaration of love and a proposal of marriage from the man she longed to live with would put her into a mood like this? It was a good thing she didn't get proposed to very often!

Her throat knotted with nerves, she walked down the narrow corridor towards the lobby, with about as much enthusiasm as a turkey heading for the chopping block.

Paul watched her come towards him, his eyes gleaming with appreciaton he didn't trouble to hide, and already her spirits lifted. They could talk about marriage later. For the moment, just being with him was everything.

'M-m-m,' was his murmured greeting, and if he'd made a twenty-minute speech telling her how beautiful she was, it couldn't have been any more sincere or pleased her more.

'So,' he said, grinning lopsidedly down at her, 'what's the answer? Or do you want me to get down on one knee?' He tucked her hand in the crook of his arm—as always, his touch sent electric vibrations trembling through her—and led her towards the restaurant entrance. She wondered idly what would happen if she told him to get down on one knee. But that would have taken more nerve than she had.

'Well?' he said. 'This suspense is going to do me in if it keeps up much longer.' That casual, easy grin of his made it very clear just how much suspense he was in.

'Paul,' Jenny said tentatively, 'I——' But her courage failed her for this, too. She would do better to set her terms after a good dinner. 'I hardly know anything about you,' she finished lamely. Then she managed a small smile. 'Except, of course, that you always get your way.' Until now, anyway.

'*Monsieur* Brant! How marvellous to see you again!' The *maître d'*, gorgeously turned out in a tuxedo and a ruffled, lavender dress shirt that Jenny wouldn't have minded in her own wardrobe, beamed as if he'd just received a twenty-dollar tip. 'Your usual table?'

'Yes, thank you, Henri.'

Jenny couldn't help smiling. Of course Paul would be on good tems with the the *maître d'* of the Tuolomne Lodge Garden Room. Of course his 'usual' table would be waiting for him, although the restaurant was crowded and he hadn't made a reservation. Was it this way for him in all the great resorts of the world? She suspected it was.

Henri seated her with a flourish, then leaned over them with the menus, hesitating. 'Do you wish menus? Or perhaps *Monsieur* would like me to suggest——?'

'Fine, Henri.'

'Ah, very well.' Henri looked as if he'd been granted the greatest favour of his life. 'I would recommend the *potage au cresson* to begin, to be followed by the lobster thermidor with——'

'Whatever you think best, Henri. We're in your hands completely.'

Henri's smile was dazzling. 'Of course, *Monsieur*. I'll take care of it. I will send the wine steward——'

'Not necessary, Henri. We'll trust your judgement.'

'Ah, then I would say a pale sherry to start, a Muscadet with the soup, and with the lobster a more full-bodied white, a Graves . . .'

'That sounds perfect.'

Henri bustled off, glowing with pleasure.

It occurred to Jenny that in the next-to-impossible event of Paul agreeing to her terms, she might demand one other minor concession: that he grant her the intelligence to decide for herself what she wanted to eat. Tonight, however, she couldn't get very irritated about it. He hadn't even chosen for himself. He had hurried through the ordering, it seemed to her, because he wanted to talk.

He looked at her, his eyes abruptly grave and sober. 'Jenny,' he said seriously, 'we're going to be sharing our lives from now on, so I want to level with you about myself. What you think about me is wrong.'

'Paul, remember, I haven't said I'm willing ... What do you mean, what I think about you is wrong?'

'I *don't* always get my way.' He toyed with his stemmed water glass, oddly uneasy. 'I didn't get the thing I wanted most out of life.'

Jenny was suddenly uneasy, too. Her stomach churned uncomfortably. She sipped her water nervously. 'Was it ... a woman?' she asked softly.

Paul seemed to come out of a brief, sombre reverie of his own. He looked at her blankly. 'Was *what* a woman?'

'The thing you wanted most in life?'

He smiled; a ghost of his usual frank grin. 'Talk about female vanity! No, as a matter of fact it wasn't a woman.' The smile widened into something like the old grin. 'Never had too much trouble getting those.'

The wine steward brought their sherries in thin, fluted glasses. She watched Paul take a reflective sip and prayed he would go on this time, and not do a rerun of his clam routine.

'In a way,' he mused, 'I suppose the whole miserable business did cost me my fiancée, but that was incidental, really.'

'What whole business?' she prompted, barely

daring to breathe.

'A perforated ear-drum.'

She very nearly laughed; she had been expecting some sinister, colossal secret—but a perforated ear-drum? It wasn't something one enjoyed, but it wasn't the end of the world, either. Her sister Gail had broken her ear-drum in a trampoline accident when she was eight, and aside from a few weeks of partial deafness and discomfort it hadn't affected her in the least.

Fortunately, she didn't laugh. The tensing of a muscle in his jaw and a sudden, harsh flare in his eyes stopped her.

'A simple, lousy, broken ear-drum.' He jerked his head angrily. 'Sometimes I still can't believe that anything that small could stand between me and everything I'd ever worked towards ... dreamed about ...'

At her puzzled frown his look gentled, and he smiled again. 'You know, no one's ever got me to talk about it before—although you came pretty close, up on Goat Peak—so I know I'm not expressing myself very clearly. You see, I was going to follow the Brant tradition and become a pilot—I mean a professional one.'

He took another sip of sherry. 'It's quite a tradition. With all the money we've got, my family's always been able to do pretty much whatever they want. My grandfather flew in the first war and my father in the second. I have an uncle who put on barnstorming exhibitions in the forties, and another one who flew a mail run in the thirties. My older brother Phil's a Navy pilot. So naturally, I wanted to be a pilot, too.'

He glanced at her suddenly. 'Do you think this sounds silly?'

Jenny wasn't yet sure what she thought, but if it was important to Paul, then it was important to her. 'No,' she said, 'of course not.' She tasted her own sherry without even knowing it, waiting for him to go on.

'I idolised Phil,' he continued dreamily, 'so when I was a kid, all I thought about was being a Navy pilot, too. But I had it all figured out how I was going to take the tradition a few steps further. After a few years of flying fighter jets, I knew I'd have what it took to become a test pilot, and then . . .'

His laugh was hollow and humourless, like a hopeless cry. Jenny wanted to hug him.

'And then I'd become the *first* Brant astronaut. Sounds pretty dumb, doesn't it?'

'No——'

'I had it all, Jenny,' he said, his voice low, intense, and bitter. 'Flying's in my blood—it's all my father ever hoped for for me—and I had the brains, the nerve . . . And then, just a few weeks after I'd gotten my degree in aerospace engineering, I got a cold. A *cold*, can you believe it?' He drained his sherry, shrugged, and went on with less emotion. 'And that was that. I'd already applied for officer's training school, but it was all over. Somehow, my middle ear got infected, the ear-drum ruptured, and that was that. You don't fly jets for Uncle Sam unless your *membrana tympani* is in one smooth piece.'

Jenny leaned back with a long sigh. So this was what Paul Brant was all about! Clearly, the shattering of the dream he had grown up with, by so ridiculously trivial an injury, had dictated everything that had

come after, had perverted his innate, pent-up courage
and his need for challenge into a wild testing of fate—
a battle against fate, really, and one that he couldn't
possibly win. No one ever won against fate.

She was silent for almost a minute, trying to
imagine the devastation he must have felt. Then she
reached out to touch the back of his hand. 'How awful
that must have been, Paul . . . but still, there must be a
thousand useful, challenging things you could——'

With two fingers he pressed her lips gently closed.
'Uh—uh,' he said, 'no platitudes, please. I've heard
them all, believe me.'

'But——' she tried to say.

He shook his head. 'Nope.' His eyes had grown
playful and relaxed. It had eased him to tell her about
it, and the thought warmed her. 'All right,' he said,
'I've given you my deep, dark secret. Now let's hear
yours.'

'Mine? But I don't have one.'

'Come on, Jenny.' He smiled patiently, keeping his
eyes on hers.

When she was a little girl, her father had claimed
that by fixing a certain, searching gaze on her eyes, he
could always tell when she was holding something
back, and she had eventually come to believe him.
That was the kind of look in Paul's green eyes now,
and it made her feel the same way. Well, not exactly
the same.

And before she knew it she was telling him about
Jim. How they had practically grown up together.
How they were to be married the summer after she
graduated from high school.

The flow of conversation was interrupted from

time to time by the appearance of Henri with their
food. She was vaguely aware that the soup was like
liquid velvet, the lobster's sauce a heavenly combination of cream, sherry, and mushrooms, but she
could have been eating a warmed-up TV dinner for
all it mattered. Or even one straight out of the freezer.
Nothing mattered but the lovely knowledge that Paul
and she were sharing private things about themselves,
things they had never shared with anyone else. Only
when she finally got to the accident—to her 'deep,
dark secret'—did her voice falter.

'He didn't want to go for a drive that night after the
party. But I did, and I made him go. We had a
favourite turn-out along Pinery Canyon Road where
you could see all the way to the lights of Wilcox.
Sometimes even the glow from Tucson.'

'And?' Paul said after a moment.

She sipped her wine without knowing it. 'We never
made it. Jim took a turn too fast and we went over the
edge.'

'I think I'm beginning to see why you don't like cars
and speed,' he murmured gently.

'The car landed upside down in a ravine,' she went
on woodenly. 'I told people later that the first thing I
remembered was getting taken out of the wreckage—
they had to pull me through the window—but I
wasn't telling the truth. I was conscious the whole
time, lying there, upside down . . . I could see Jim was
. . . was dead. He was all——' She shut her eyes, as if
that could shut out the dreadful memory. 'We were
there for *five hours*, Paul!' she said in a strangled voice.

'My God,' Paul said, and now it was his turn to reach
for her hand. 'You poor kid.'

'Five hours,' she repeated slowly, 'and I was conscious, looking at him, knowing that it was my fault, that if not for me he'd still be——'

'What nonsense!' he said so abruptly that she started. 'You made a mistake not talking about it a long time ago. It wouldn't have taken a psychiatrist to tell you it wasn't any more your fault than his. Less. You weren't driving.'

'But don't you see, we'd had some drinks. I never should have made him go. But it seemed like fun— exciting, dangerous—to go speeding up the canyon at midnight.' She picked listlessly at her napkin. 'Fun!'

'I see,' Paul drawled, 'so you were the wild one and Jim was the quiet, timid sort, and you egged him on until you killed him. Is that it?'

'Well, not exactly,' Jenny had to say, trying to present it honestly. 'I guess Jim was as wild as I was, but that's beside the point. He wouldn't have gone that night if I hadn't called him a wet blanket. That was the straw that did it.'

Paul winced. 'Ouch! I'm starting to understand a lot of things.' He squeezed her hand. 'But you're not looking at it right. Don't get me wrong; I'm not excusing you. I'm just saying he gets as much blame as you do. You keep saying that you *made* him go? What's that supposed to mean? Did you *force* him to go? Did you threaten to kill him if he didn't?'

'No——'

'Did you tell him you'd never see him again if he didn't?'

'No, of course not . . .' It was strange. She saw what Paul was getting at, but she was fighting him, as if she didn't want to let go of the grief and guilt she'd nursed for so long. 'I just . . . well, I just told him I wanted to go, that's all.'

'And he went of his own free will.'

'But——'

'Jenny,' he said, so quietly that she had to lean forward to hear him, 'the things we do to ourselves we do *by* ourselves. Nobody else can be responsible for our actions. You didn't *make* Jim get into that car, any more than Jim's death *made* you draw into yourself the way you did, and pour all your energies into search-and-rescue. For whatever we do with our life, we're the ones who deserves the blame. And the credit. You've saved a lot of people's lives since then.'

She looked at him thoughtfully. How very right he was! How cowardly she'd been, in a way, to refuse to face herself, to take responsibility for herself. 'You're right,' she said. 'And thank you for saying it.'

A slow smile spread across her face. 'I think that goes for ear-drums, too,' she added softly.

'Ear-drums?' he echoed, puzzled.

'Broken ear-drums don't make us do things, either. We're responsible for our own actions, Paul.'

'Well, yes but——' He burst into laughter. '*Touché*. And not only *touché*, but you're absolutely right.' He held up his wine glass and clinked it against hers. 'You know, we're going to be very good for each other. You've made a wise decision, marrying me.'

Oops, she'd forgotten all about that! But this wasn't the time; this wasn't the time at all. She was glowing with happiness, and she wasn't going to spoil the moment. Time enough later—and maybe, considering the way the talk had gone, it might be, it just might be, that there was a chance that he'd see reason, that there was going to be a happy ending to all this, after all. But later.

She laughed and touched glasses with him again. 'Who's this fiancée you mentioned? Someone you met in college?'

'That's another long story.' Paul tossed his white cloth napkin on the table. 'If you really want to hear chapter and verse, let's have our coffee sent up to my suite, so we can be comfortable. These chairs are *hard*.'

Comfortable meant lighting the logs in the fireplace with the long matchsticks thoughtfully provided, turning on some quiet music, and sinking blissfully back against the soft cushions of the sofa, perfectly placed for watching the snapping orange flames. Once the room service waiter had left, they kicked off their shoes and put their feet up on the coffee table. Paul had been right. This was much more comfortable, indeed.

After Paul discarded his tie and loosened his shirt collar, it seemed perfectly natural for him to put his arm around her and for her to snuggle up against him, her cheek resting in the valley between his shoulder and his chin.

Paul's hand moved caressingly up and down her arm, deliciously slowly. 'Now what were we talking about?'

'Your ex-fiancée,' Jenny answered, although she couldn't honestly say the subject fascinated her at the moment, or that she really felt much like talking at all. It was very pleasant lying quietly against him, staring into the bright, warm fire, feeling the hypnotic, rhythmic movement of his stroking hand.

'Right, my ex-fiancée.' He didn't seem much more

enthusiastic about this than she did. 'Yes, I met her in college. Her father was also an Air Force officer, and she worshipped him. That's what she wanted for me, too. We got engaged during my senior year. But then, when I flunked the physical, well . . .'

'You mean she broke it off just because you couldn't be an officer?' Jenny said incredulously. She would have thought Paul Conan Brant, ordinary civilian, would have been pretty heady stuff for any woman.

He shrugged and she felt the play of the firm muscles beneath her cheek. She found her fingers toying with the top button of his shirt. How easy it would be, how lovely . . .

'Not exactly,' Paul said. 'It was more of a mutual decison. She tried to make the best of it, but she couldn't hide her disappointment any more than I could. So we put things off for a year. I tried to get my head back on straight by sailing the Atlantic . . .'

'And got caught in a storm, and blown off course, and you were presumed drowned.'

'You read about that?' He seemed surprised.

'It was pretty hard not to; you make terrific press copy.'

'Well, I always try to be entertaining. Anyway, it didn't take her long to find somebody to console her, and by the time I popped up again, she was happily re-engaged.'

'To an Air Force pilot?'

'To the president of a bakery chain. Still very happy, I understand.' He laughed, and Jenny joined him.

'And that's it? That's the long story?' She glanced at her wrist watch. 'That took all of sixty seconds. We could have stayed in the restaurant.'

'Ah, but I had an ulterior motive.' He tilted her
chin up so he could look into her eyes, and the old,
familiar shivers trickled icily down her spine. 'I
wanted to talk about us, and I didn't want to do it
from the other side of a table.'

'Talk?' she whispered shakily.

He nodded. 'About us.'

But he didn't talk. He seemed to be as lost in her
eyes as she was in his. 'My God, I love you!' he
whispered fiercely.

His mouth descended slowly on hers while their
eyes were still locked. The steady, insistent power of it
couldn't be resisted, even if she'd wanted to. His eyes
closed under knotted brows, and Jenny had a sudden,
joyful sense of her own power. And then of her
weakness. Her eyes closed too, and her arms wound
themselves tightly around his neck. She opened her
lips, and his tongue burst in, exploring, probing. She
gasped and pushed her mouth even harder against his.
She needed him so desperately . . . needed to be even
closer, closer . . .

He responded with growing passion. Jenny could
feel his heartbeat accelerate. His strong hands moved
from her face down her throat, and then down the
length of her body, and suddenly, somehow, she was
lying full-length on the sofa with him beside her. He
stroked, then cupped a breast in one hand, and pressed
his face down to it, through the cloth. A passion like
nothing she had ever felt before, stunning in its
intensity, leaped up in her. With her hand in his hair
she pressed his face even harder against her breast.
Her body arched instinctively towards him, and she

heard herself moan, a soft, strange whimper she
hadn't known she was capable of.

Paul's hands were at her hips, pulling her closer still
to his hot body. He too was moaning and breathless.
His lips were at her throat, her chin, her mouth. They
found themselves suddenly looking directly into each
other's eyes again, and, surprisingly, they both
laughed and pulled their faces apart, gasping for
breath.

'Do you always kiss with your eyes open?' he said.

'No. That is, I don't think so. I never thought about
it before.'

They lay side by side, looking at each other, their
heads on the same small sofa cushion. Paul's head was
outlined by the fire's luminescence.

'Jenny, Jenny,' he murmured. 'I do love you. I don't
think you have any idea how special you are.'

'You know, I'm beginning to believe you really
mean it.' She laughed, but the sound was shaky, and
tears trembled on her lashes. If her heart got any fuller
it was going to burst.

'About time.' He dropped a small kiss on her
forehead, and then one on each lowered eyelid.

But it wasn't her eyelids that Jenny wanted kissed;
she was well past that. With a force and boldness that
must have surprised him—it certainly astonished
her—she pulled his face down to hers and hungrily
kissed his mouth again, and then again. And it was her
hand that did the exploring this time; into the neck of
his shirt, her palm against the hard, curving muscles
of his chest, her fingers in the curling hair.

To her surprise, he drew back a little and grasped
her wrist, pulling her hand from his shirt.

'Whoa, there!' He laughed unsteadily, caught her other hand too, and held them both in his. 'Hold it. I'm barely in control now, and I want to talk something out before things get serious.'

'You don't call this serious?' Jenny said lightly, but a tiny pinpoint of fear pricked the pit of her stomach and she lay still, her breath caught in her throat.

'Come on, sit up,' he said, and pulled her up by her hands. 'This is no position in which to have a sober discussion.' There was still some coffee left in the pot and he poured some for both of them. Jenny had no desire for coffee, but she drank some anyway.

'Your hair seems to be mussed,' he said with a smile.

'I wonder why.' Nervously, she brushed it more or less into place with her hand. What did he want to talk about?

Paul leaned forward, towards the fire, his elbows on his knees, the cup held in both hands. The flames had died down now, and in the dull, flickering glow his face was like polished copper.

'All right. First of all, I know how you feel about the risks I take. And I admit I do some pretty dumb things.' He turned his head towards her. 'By the way, I probably ought to tell you that I half-expected you to deliver some kind of ultimatum when I asked you to marry me. You know: "Give up your reckless ways or live without me for ever more." That kind of thing.'

The coffee went down the wrong pipe, and Jenny only barely kept from spluttering. 'I wouldn't think of it,' she said in a small voice.

'Good. Other women have tried it. I guess I should have know you wouldn't.'

'Of course not,' she said, not quite daring to meet

his eyes. 'What a ridiculous idea. Paul, what did you want to talk through?'

He smiled and turned to the fire agian, his voice soft. 'You know, Jenny, I'd gotten to the stage where even risking my life had become pretty pale. When I ran into trouble in Bert's ultralight, I figured I'd had it; Paul Brant's life was over.' He stared down at his cup. 'I can't say that I gave much of a damn.'

Again he turned to look at her, almost shyly. 'But I wasn't dead. I opened my eyes, and there you were. And suddenly I wanted to live again—I *needed* to live.' A slow, crooked smile lifted one side of his mouth. 'Sounds pretty corny, I guess.'

Not to Jenny it didn't! It was the most beautiful, most fantastic thing she'd ever heard. Too filled with emotion to speak, she lay her hand on his. The tears glided openly down her cheeks, but she didn't wipe them away.

'And since then,' he went on in the same slow, thoughtful voice, 'the world's seemed like a good place again. It's made sense again. And not just because I fell in love with you—although that helped—but because you taught me something important . . .'

'Paul . . . Paul . . .' she whispered, bursting with joy, simply needing to say his name.

'You taught me that there are other kinds of adventure besides sitting in a jet cockpit or playing Russian roulette. There's *useful* adventure, too; that week in the mountains proved I have skills that can save people's lives——'

'Of course you do!' she bubbled, finally dabbing at her eyes with the back of her hand. She laughed, still crying.

'More than that,' he said, with a little sparkle in his eyes, 'it was a hell of a lot of fun.' He put down the cup and held her hand in both of his. 'Jenny, I just want you to know that you won't be marrying an aimless loafer or anything like it. I want to start doing something constructive with my life again. And I mean to do it.'

Jenny expelled her breath with a rush. She kept thinking it was impossible to get any happier, and then she kept getting happier. 'Oh, Paul, how I love you!' she cried, and flung her arms around his neck. 'I——'

But again he pulled back, and firmly unwound them. 'No, wait, let me finish. I haven't said what I need to say.'

Again the pinprick of fear; smaller this time, but enough to make her heartbeat hesitate disquietingly.

'Well, the thing is—oh, hell, this isn't any easier than I thought it would be.'

'What, Paul?' she said without expression, not letting herself even try to imagine what he was going to say. 'Tell me.'

He picked up his coffee again. It had to be cold by now, but he swallowed some, anyway. 'Last summer, before I had any idea Jenny Roberts existed, I made a commitment for a climb in May. The men I'm climbing with have already started training, and I'm not about to back out now. I just wanted you to know about it, and to know that——'

'Where?' she said, her voice wooden.

He didn't pretend to misunderstand her or evade the question. 'Here. Yosemite.'

'What are you climbing, Half-Dome?' Please let it

be Half-Dome, she prayed. For a climber of Paul's calibre it would be a snap.

'No. The Big Wall.'

The very sound of the words made her stomach sink even further. 'The what?'

'Sorry. Climbers' jargon for El Capitan.'

'El Capitan! Paul, even I know about El Capitan! It's the most dangerous climb there is! There aren't any ledges, there are hardly any handholds—it's just three thousand feet straight up!'

'Not quite straight,' he said with a grin. 'Near the top it slants *outwards* into an overhang, so——'

'Paul, it's not funny!'

'Jenny . . .' He reached for her hand but she pulled sharply back. She brushed her hair from her eyes, so sick she could hardly speak. 'You can't!' she said without thinking. 'I won't let you!'

His face hardened instantly. 'You what?' he said through compressed lips.

'I—I'm sorry, I didn't mean that,' she said, beginning to feel the feathery, fluttering touch of panic. Her lovely new world was splintering, collapsing. 'It's just that . . . a single mistake, a single piece of faulty equipment and you'd be dead.'

Paul's forehead creased. His eyes had turned hard, too. 'I'm not exactly a novice, you know. Everest wasn't the easiest——'

'Everest at least has *ledges* to sleep on,' she cut in angrily. 'What will you do on El Capitan? Drive a couple of pitons in and hang a hammock on them? And don't tell me you can climb that thing in a single day!'

'No,' he said evenly, 'it takes ten, but——'

Jenny jumped up. '*Ten?*' She stared at him incredulously. Something like a strangled laugh escaped from her throat. The five hours trapped in the car with Jim had been an endless, horrible eternity. To even imagine ... No, it was unthinkable. 'Ten days! You——'

'Will you shut up for a minute?' He stood up and grasped her by the arms so she couldn't turn away from him. 'Now listen to me,' he said icily. 'Compared to Everest——'

She twisted away. 'I don't want to hear about Everest. I didn't know you then, and even if I did and you'd failed, I wouldn't have had to *watch* you die!'

Paul rolled his eyes ceilingward and let out an exasperated sigh. 'What are you talking about? In the first place, who's going to die? And in the second place, I don't want you anywhere near Yosemite during the climb.' He smiled, willing to make a move towards smoothing things over. 'It would throw off my concentration something awful!' He took her by the arm again. 'Now come here, and let's——'

Angrily, she shook him off. 'I wouldn't need to be here. The word will get out that you're climbing, and some television station will cover it. If you—if you fall, it will be all over the media.' She brushed absently at a sudden new flow of tears. 'Paul, it's not fair to make me go through this. You say you love me—you say you're going to change. Well, why not do it *now*? It's not too late to get out of it, is it?'

This time he was silent, turning away from her to stare broodingly into the dying, hissing fire. The set of his shoulders told her all she needed to know.

After a long moment he spoke, not looking up.

'You're exaggerating all of this, you know,' he said impassively, 'and you're not being terrifically rational. If——'

'Rational!' she echoed, then stopped, her throat clogged with a hundred conflicting emotions.

She saw his shoulders lift, then fall in a long, silent breath, while he continued to stare down at the embers. 'It's not a question of whether it's too late to get out of it. I gave my word, people are counting on me, and——' He turned his head slowly towards her, his eyes the eyes of a stranger. '——and I'm going.'

He couldn't have spoken more softly, or with less anger, but the words—and his eyes, the eyes that had looked at her with so much love such a little while ago—turned her heart to ice. It was all over; the bubble had burst. It had turned out to be just one more sweet, agonising dream, and now it was time to wake up.

She had only a vague memory of the rest of the ugly argument, and of how they went over the same ground again and again. But Paul knew as well as she did that there couldn't be any resolution, and in the end, weary and drained of all feeling, they agreed they were at an impasse and talking about it any more wasn't going to help. But she had a very clear memory of how cold the brass handle felt when she opened the door, and how, when she'd left without looking back, she knew that she had left her happiness lying in meaningless, shattered fragments behind her.

CHAPTER NINE

WOULD he have believed it if someone had told him a few years ago that the prospect of climbing El Capitan would leave him more apathetic than anything else? Not likely. Apathetic, indifferent . . . bored. In short, he just didn't give a damn!

Paul poked listlessly at the smouldering logs in the fireplace, then drained his Scotch and set the glass down with a thump on the table beside the armchair. The hell with it, he thought stolidly, I'm here and I'll see it through. I owe it to the rest of the team; they're counting on me. He reached for the bottle and poured himself another drink. Methodically working your way through a fifth of whisky was no way to spend the night before a demanding ten-day climb, and he knew it. If he had any sense, he would be doing what the other team members were doing right now, which was snoring away in their rooms. But who had ever said he had any sense? Anyway, he had the others so rigorously drilled by now, they could make it even if he figured out a way to stay drunk all ten days on the Wall.

So, the hell with it . . .

He seemed to be saying that to himself a lot these days. 'Women,' he muttered aloud, staring bleakly into the orange glow of the fire. How smug he'd been all these years, thinking he knew what made them tick! He allowed himself a small smile. Well, he knew *some* of what made them tick, but not all. Not by a long shot.

When he had failed to get that Air Force commission he'd built his life around, he thought he'd hit rock bottom, but that was nothing compared to this. Never in his life had he felt so extravagantly empty, so cruelly aware that his life was a meaningless joke, hollow and pointless. Without Jenny, what did any of it matter? The first woman in his life he had ever needed—truly *needed*, in every sense of the word there was—and he'd ruined his chance.

Oh, he'd been so sure of himself, so certain of his ability to handle a young and impressionable female who had clearly been bedazzled when the celebrated Paul Conan Brant came striding manfully into her life. Well, crashing into it, but at least it was a novel approach. And how wrong he had been—it served him right for believing his own Press notices. All through these last weeks, he'd continued to expect her to come around to his way of thinking. She'd just needed some time to calm down, he had confidently told himself. Well, seven weeks had gone by, and he was still waiting. And if she was waiting for *him* to swallow his pride and come crawling, he thought grimly, then she——

The telephone's ring made him start. He'd left explicit instructions at the desk: no telephone calls, except from . . . He stared at it, his heart lifting for the first time in days. Maybe he just might swallow his pride after all, given a little encouragement. On the third ring he put down the Scotch, and lifted the receiver, his breath painfully short.

The voice was male, smooth, unfamiliar. 'Mr Brant——'

'Who is this?' Paul grated. 'How the hell did you get through?'

'This is Ben Thornton, ABS-TV. They told me at the desk that you're not taking any calls, but——'

'They told you right.'

'Wait, don't hang up, Mr Brant. Look, I've got a national hook-up arranged from Yosemite for tomorrow morning's *Hello, USA* show, and——'

'No!'

'I beg your pardon?'

'No.'

'Mr Brant,' Thornton said, a hint of irritation showing through, 'your climb doesn't start until the afternoon, so there's plenty of time, and remember, we're talking national exposure here——'

'Fine, do it without me.'

'Now just a minute, friend, people don't go around saying "no" to *Hello, USA*——'

'Well, I just said it. Goodnight.'

'Look, maybe you didn't understand who this is. This is Ben——'

Paul slammed the receiver down, but by the time he had refilled his glass, he was feeling contrite and a little ashamed of himself. He'd never been the most patient guy in the world, God knows, but he'd always been basically civil. Thornton had only been doing his job, after all, and there hadn't been any need to be rude to him. He reached for the telephone again; he owed the man an apology. And there wasn't really any reason why he couldn't spare half an hour for a TV interview ...

But somehow he couldn't summon the motivation to call the desk and get the number for ABS.

He replaced the telephone and settled slowly back in the chair, Scotch in hand.

The hell with it . . .

'Paul Conan Brant III Faces Crack of Doom.'

The headline alone was enough to turn her blood to ice, but of course she kept on reading.

Paul Conan Brant III and three companions today received final permission from Yosemite National Park authorities to begin their historic assault on mighty El Capitan late Thursday afternoon with a short climb to their first rest-stop. The three-thousand foot granite monolith is generally considered by experts to present North America's premier rock-climbing challenge. Brant's team will try to establish a new route, more dangerous than any accomplished heretofore, and believed by many to be impossible.

In order to gain the summit, Brant and his team will have to negotiate several of El Capitan's most terryfying features: the huge vertical fissures and weaknesses that mar the seemingly sheer surface. Over the years they have been named by awed mountaineers—the Crack of Doom, the Crack of Despair, the Widow Maker—and their grim histories make clear the reasons for the names.

The normally outgoing and sociable Brant has been in virtual seclusion at Tuolomne Lodge,

unavailable to the Press and refusing all telephone calls, and a source close to the team says
that there is some concern over his uncharacter-
istically moody and ill-tempered attitude ...

The tense ache at the back of her neck seemed
suddenly to condense and settle behind her eyes. She
closed them, unable to read any more, and dropped
the *Phoenix Sun* back on the end table in the employees'
lounge. Thursday. Today. She stood up abruptly.
Hardly aware of what she was doing, she poured out
her untouched coffee, rinsed her mug, and hung it on
a hook in the cupboard.

She had barely opened her teller's window when
the rhythmic jangle of coins made her look up. Mr
Rayburn was unlocking the door and the first
customer, Ed Burnaby, was clanking his way in with
yesterday's proceeds from the laundry. It was odd—
and disturbing: every time Ed came in, Jenny
thought of Paul. Of how she had looked over the old
man's shoulder that day and seen him smiling,
waiting to ask her to dinner. Of how she wished she
could take time back and look over Ed's shoulder
and see him now, and have the chance to try it all
again ...

But in the seven miserable weeks since the trip to
Yosemite she hadn't seen or heard from him once.
That had been her fault, mostly, for when she
discovered that Paul, instead of flying off to parts
unknown as she had fully expected, had continued to
run Lyre Creek Ranch and to participate in the rescue
team, Jenny had cowardly suspended her own

membership. And plunged into an even deeper depression.

Jenny's smile was summoned with effort. She liked Ed, but a gossipy chat was the last thing she wanted now. And if he sang out his invariable 'How's my favourite banker?', she was going to hit him with one of his own coin sacks.

He didn't. He was too busy muttering under his breath.

'Is something wrong, Ed?' she asked, her own troubles pushed to the background for a moment.

'You're darn right,' he said, plunking the sacks on the counter with a sigh of exasperation. 'It's my brother Albert, that old fool . . .'

Jenny listened as attentively as she could to Ed's confusing story of a quarrel with his brother. What with stacking and counting quarters and dimes, she never did get straight exactly what they were arguing over, except that it had something to do with the disposition of an antique whisky flask that Ed thought should go to the County Historical Society, and his brother maintained should go elsewhere. But knowing both men, it wasn't difficult to guess where the problem lay. They had each painted themselves into a verbal corner and were too proud and too stubborn to admit it.

'I wonder if part of the problem between you and Albert is that you're too much alike,' she said, giving him his receipt.

'Me?' His shaggy eyebrows shot up incredulously. 'Like that mule-headed . . .?'

Whatever the rest was, Jenny never heard it. Her own words boomeranged back at her. They'd done more than that; they had opened a locked door and thrown an inescapable light on her unuttered and half-apprehended broodings.

She stood there as if turned to stone, realising with a sudden, crashing despair that she was more in the wrong than Paul was—that it was she, not he, who had wielded the brush that had forced her into her wretched, lonely corner. What a terrible fool she'd been—proud, self-centred, childish—all the things she had accused him of. The only man she loved, ever would love, and she'd flung his proposal back in his teeth! And now——

Now it was too late. It was over. She'd had her chance; she'd had seven weeks of chances, and she had stubbornly, stupidly clung to her pride. Well, she still had her pride, but what else did she have? She'd waited one day too long, she thought bitterly. He wasn't even accepting phone calls. If only he weren't climbing until tomorrow, or if she'd come to her senses yesterday instead of today, she would still have a chance to reach him before he started. But now, that was impossible.

And it would be so much wasted breath if she tried to tell him *after* his climb that she loved him more than enough to take him as he was. He would laugh at her, she realised, blinking back tears, and who could blame him?

Or was it too late? The thought burgeoned slowly, like a blossoming flower. 'Late afternoon,' the newspaper had said. What time was 'late afternoon'? It wasn't yet ten in the morning; if she got to the airport near Tucson by eleven, maybe, just maybe . . .

'. . . Really miss! I've been waiting in line for fifteen

minutes, and if you can't at least have the courtesy . . .'

She realised with surprise that Ed wasn't there any more, and the irritated words were directed at her.

'I . . . I'm sorry,' she stammered. 'I . . . I have to go.'

And before the dumbfounded gazes of customers and tellers she dashed from her work station. She actually ran into an astounded Mr Rayburn, but simply kept going. What did any of it matter? There was only one thing that counted: could she get there in time? Was it possible?

That and the other thing. When she got there, would Paul even care? Seven weeks was a long time, and Paul Brant was not a patient man. She prayed he was a forgiving one.

Getting to Yosemite National Park from Cochise Bend without Paul's plane at her disposal was a gruelling trip: an hour's drive to the Tucson Airport, a fortuitously scheduled United flight to Los Angeles, a hectic dash through the immense LA airport to catch—barely—an AirCal hop to Merced—the only one that gave her even a ghost of a chance to get there before 'late afternoon', whenever that was. And finally a Greyhound bus to Yosemite.

Not one miserable leg of it went smoothly. Even without taking the time to stop at her apartment, she hadn't made it to Tucson in time to park her station wagon in the long-term car park and catch her flight. She'd wound up leaving it in the yellow unloading zone in front of the terminal, knowing full well it would be towed away and impounded—lord knew where—and she would have to pay a walloping fine to get it back.

That was only the beginning. Both flights were delayed, the first by ten minutes, and the second by fifteen, while Jenny writhed with impatience and frustration. The bus drive had been the worst of all, because by the time they'd reached El Portal she knew that, even with all her desperate hurry, she wasn't going to make it. A spring electrical storm had slowed the bus to a wretched start-and-stop crawl through the Sierra foothills, so agonising that she almost jumped out and ran, just to be doing *something*. A 'late afternoon starting time' could mean three o'clock, or even four o'clock. But not five. Or could it?

By the time she got to Tuolomne Lodge she was practically weeping with tension. She had caught a glimpse of El Capitan as the bus drove by it on its way to the lodge, but her view was obscured by the huge trees along the roadway, and it was impossible to tell anything. She approached the desk trembling, her heart in her mouth.

'Has Paul Brant left yet?'

To her surprise, the desk manager recognised her. 'Yes, Miss Roberts. I'm afraid you missed him.'

'When——?'

'He checked out at noon.'

'*Noon!*' Jenny felt as if her legs might fail under her. She gripped the edge of the reception desk. Her throat swelled and tightened; it was a struggle to get the words out. 'Noon,' she breathed. 'But—when did he start the climb?'

'Three o'clock; two hours ago.' Raymond took a closer look at Jenny's face and leaned forward. 'Is something wrong, Miss Roberts? Can I do something for you?'

Unable to speak, Jenny shook her head and turned blindly away. She had lost the gamble. A hundred immediate concerns nibbled at her mind. She was eight hundred miles from home, with one dollar and seventy-five cents in cash and a credit card that was charged to the limit—and then some, after today's flight. Her poor car was impounded in some haul-away lot near Tucson, her job was probably a thing of the past, she had no change of clothes with her, no toothbrush, no idea where she would spend the night. And she hadn't eaten since breakfast.

The dreary litany went on, but she couldn't bring herself to care very much about any of it; it would all work out somehow. Only one thing wouldn't work out, but that was the only thing that mattered——

For the second time that day she walked unseeingly into someone.

'I'm sorry,' she murmured, and pushed gently against the tall figure to disentangle herself.

But he didn't give ground quite the way Mr Rayburn had. He stood firm. Two powerful hands gripped her arms and held her motionless.

'Jenny? Is it really you?' Paul's voice was urgent and weary, husky and familiar.

For several seconds she was numb, disbelieving what her senses told her. Then, all at once, she was clinging to him with every ounce of strength she had, needing desperately to feel his body pressed against her, to have his arms, warm and alive and possessive around her. *Is is really you?* he had asked, and in all her fantasies, nothing she had dreamed he might say could have sounded sweeter.

He held her even tighter than she held him, and it

was bliss to have the breath driven from her. After a few moments she stepped back, but he kept his hands on her arms as if he were afraid she might disappear again.

'Let's get out of here.'

Dazed, Jenny could only nod. With Paul she crossed the lobby, hardly noticing the bemused stares and raised eyebrows of the people who had watched their meeting. They had walked the long, lushly carpeted corridor to his suite before she found her voice, and then the words wouldn't stop.

'The desk manager—Raymond—said you were gone, that I'd missed you. He said that—that you'd already started the climb—that you started at three o'clock, that . . .'

He was shaking his head, smiling softly. 'No.'

'But——' Her eyes widened. 'Do you mean that you've decided——'

'Not to make the climb?' He didn't move, but it seemed as if he had suddenly pulled back, far away from her, The cold, jadelike gleam of anger that she'd seen so often in his eyes flared ominously. 'Is that why you've come?' His voice was flat. 'Is this a last-ditch try to get me to change my mind? If it is, you're wasting——'

'No,' she cried hastily, 'that isn't why I came! Honestly!'

'The reason I'm not up there now,' he said evenly, 'is that that electrical storm has put off the start. That's the only reason, Jenny. Tomorrow afternoon, I go.'

Jenny felt her nerve slipping away before that smouldering gaze, but this was the time to say what she'd come to say. 'Paul, I came to tell you that I was wrong to . . . to ask you to go back on your word, to back down on a commitment—and my only excuse is that I love you so terribly much that I was afraid of what it would do to me if I lost you.' She licked her dry lips. 'And . . . and to . . .' Her courage failed her.

His voice softened. 'And to what?'

She took a deep, trembling breath. 'And to see if you still love me and . . .' Afraid to look at him, she lowered her eyes. '. . . And want to marry me.'

Paul's eyes warmed to a tender, liquid glow. He took a step towards her, but stopped abruptly. Again the iron shutters slid down over his gaze.

'When?' he asked expressionlessly. 'When I've come back down?'

'No,' Jenny said, shaking her head emphatically. 'No, now! Tomorrow morning! Reno's not far away, Paul. We could get married and be back before——'

It was all she managed to get out before his arms pulled her crushingly to him. He seemed to tower far above her, looking down from a great height, his eyes alight with a brilliant, bone-melting flame of open desire. And of love.

'Paul . . . oh, Paul . . .'

He kissed her so deeply and longingly that her last fears drained harmlessly away. Jenny twined her arms around his neck as tightly as she could and strained against him, exulting in the passion that trembled and vibrated through her body, knowing that it matched his.

She caught her breath with surprise as he bent unexpectedly and swung her up into his arms, then turned towards the bedroom.

'Paul—Paul, wait! You look terrible——'

'Thanks a lot.'

'No, I mean——' She was laughing and crying at the same time. 'You look so worn out. If we're going to get married tomorrow, and you're going to climb a mountain, you need rest, you need sleep——'

'You're absolutely right,' he said, and stopped her words with his mouth. 'And hasn't anyone ever told you what the best tranquilliser in the world is? Better than sleeping pills.' He smiled down at her, his voice like velvet. 'Unless you're not in the mood of course . . .'

She smiled back at him, with her cheeks, her body, her whole world glowing, then buried her head in his shoulder while he carried her through the doorway, and then across to the wide soft bed.

She was awakened briefly just before dawn, by the first tentative stirrings of the birds in the trees outside their open windows. Paul lay on his side, his face towards hers, their foreheads touching. He raised himself on one elbow and looked down at her, his face invisible in the cool darkness.

'Are you awake?' he whispered.

'Mm-hm.'

'Look, I just want to say that it's all right with me if you'd rather wait until afterwards to get married, darling. If you'd rather have a big wedding with all the trimmings——'

'No deal,' she said, grinning up at him as her eyes grew used to the dark. 'We're getting married first thing tomorrow—I mean, today. As a new husband you'll be forced to be cautious on that stupid mountain. You're going to have responsibilities now, my good man, you'll have a wife to satisfy.'

'Mmm,' he murmured. 'Now there's a responsibility I wouldn't mind handling right now.' His warm hand ran slowly from her cheek, to her naked shoulder, to her waist, sending shuddering ripples of electricity through her as it made its way.

'Jenny . . .' He gathered her to his lean, hard body.

'Paul,' she said pushing away from him, contrary to every urge rampaging hotly through her, 'should you really—I mean, aren't you supposed to conserve your strength before a climb like El Capitan?'

'You let me worry about conserving my strength,' he laughed, and went on to demonstrate in the most pleasurable and convincing way imaginable that there wasn't anything to worry about.

EPILOGUE

'Hi, Jenny. Peg here. You guys free for dinner tonight? Bert stumbled over two pheasants when he was out hunting today——'

Jenny heard Bert's voice in the background. '*Stumbled?* It took all the ingenuity of resourceful tracking——'

She smiled as Peg continued breezily on, her husky voice drowning out Bert's aggrieved tones. '——and we're going to roast them. I've got a recipe for a port wine sauce that ought to be terrific.'

'Sounds delicious, and I'd love to come. Paul was called out yesterday, though. There was an avalanche at a ski resort in Colorado, and they needed expert reinforcements. I don't know if he'll be back in time.'

'Well, you come, anyway. But how come you got left behind?'

'Well, there's "expert" and there's "expert". Paul is an honest-to-goodness, bona-fide *expert*, as I don't have to tell you. They came for him in a light plane, and there just wasn't an extra seat for me.'

'Honestly,' Peg replied. 'It makes my head spin when I think of the life you two lead. Wasn't it a flood in Texas last week?'

'Louisiana.'

'Whatever. What's next?'

'God only knows,' Jenny answered ruefully. 'It's all I can do to keep up with him, much less predict the future—beyond pheasant and port wine sauce with my favourite neighbours tonight. And with any luck, Paul might make it back in time. I left the car at the airport for him.'

But he didn't, and it was the middle of the night before she heard the sound she had been listening for through her uneasy, on-again, off-again sleep. Yes, it was the Porsche, pulling into the driveway. She lay back on the pillows with a relieved sigh and a warm sense of expectancy. He was all right. He was back.

How strange it was. She had never had any trouble sleeping soundly by herself—until Paul came along to jumble and confuse her dreams—but now, on the nights when she had the big bed to herself, every creak and rustle woke her up and made her jittery. Yet when he was there, she never heard them, or if she did, she just snuggled up a little closer and went contentedly back to sleep in the security of his embrace.

She settled herself a little more deeply under the covers, pretending to be asleep. There were not many pretences between them, but making believe she was sleeping when he came home from a mission was one she allowed herself. Maybe she couldn't stop worrying about him, but she was certainly able to hide it. Most of the time, anyway.

Besides, she admitted frankly and happily, she loved it when he slipped quietly into bed beside her and kissed her hello. And usually there was much more than hello. A whole month of marriage, she mused dreamily, and still the simple touch of his fingers on her cheek in the night were enough to set her aflame. Or even the *thought* of his touch.

Drowsily, she listened to the welcome sounds of the garage door opening and closing, his firm step on the stairs, and then the hiss of the shower as he bathed. When she heard him switch off the bathroom light, she realised that she was holding her breath, as eager as a child on Christmas morning. She waited until she felt the whole lovely length of him stretch out next to her, and then she couldn't wait any more. She sighed his name and turned urgently towards him.

'Hello, darling,' he whispered. 'I've missed you.'

They kissed softly, three separate, brief gentle kisses: one, two, three, but the fourth was no longer so brief or so gentle. He strained hungrily against her, and, her heart swelling with happiness, she willingly pressed her own body back. The rest of the world vanished. There was nothing but Paul, nothing but his demanding mouth, his heated, thrusting body, nothing but the exquisite passion that consumed her.

Usually after they made love, he would drift off into a gentle sleep, and she loved to watch his face relax with unguarded contentment as his eyes slowly closed. But tonight he surprised her by switching on the bedside light. In its soft glow she saw a boyish, held-in excitement bubbling behind his eyes.

'They flew Peter MacCabe in on this one,' he said, casually, raising himself on one elbow and toying with a strand of her hair. 'Had a nice talk with him.'

'Peter MacCabe of the Sierra Madre team?'

'Not any more. He's just taken a job with UNDRO.'

'UNDRO.' Jenny's brow wrinkled. 'The United Nation's agency for disaster relief?'

'Yes. Headquartered in Geneva.'

'How exciting for him.' But what did this have to do

with them? What was Paul holding back?

He shrugged. 'Yes and no. Unfortunately it's a desk job, but he's willing to take it so he can put some of his ideas on disaster control to use.'

He paused, and Jenny tried to imagine what was coming next: Peter had offered him a post? Well, it would certainly be thrilling to live in Europe—for a while—but how quickly she would miss the wide-open, unpopulated spaces of the Southwest. Nevertheless, she was delighted with the way search-and-rescue work had captured Paul's imagination and stimulated that formidable intelligence of his. She'd better be. It was all her doing. Anyway, if that was what he wanted . . .

'And one of those ideas,' Paul said, and the excitement crept into his voice, 'is to form an international trouble-shooting team to get to the scene of a disaster—while it's in the making, if possible. They would be a kind of advance guard to make sure things run smoothly . . . set up command posts, co-ordinate efforts with local government, deal with unusual problems—no landing strip for aircraft, that sort of thing.'

'Don't tell me,' she said. 'He thinks you'd be a perfect candidate for the team.' Visions of cosmopolitan European living vanished before images of exploding volcanoes in South America, floods in India, earthquakes in Turkey—all with Paul right in the middle, taking terrible risks that would make climbing El Capitan seem like child's play. She reached for his hand, trying not to show the anxiety streaking through her insides like ice on the walls of a hollow cave.

He grinned. 'Let's just say he thinks I'm crazy enough to go for it. I'd only be on call, of course. There's no reason why we couldn't keep living right here.'

Instead of answering, Jenny took her hand from his, sat up, tucked her hair behind her ears, and rested her chin on her drawn-up knees. Objecting to pointless risk-taking was one thing, but how could she quarrel with this? Even though her heart was already leaden with worry for him, just thinking about it.

'Look honey,' he said quietly, his hand massaging the back of her neck, 'I know there's some danger involved, but this is my chance to do something really meaningful with my life; to put what skills I have to genuine use. Besides, it isn't really that dangerous. That's the point of what I'd be doing: to minimise the risks and dangers.'

She lifted her head from her knees and took a deep breath. There was only one antidote for worry: action. 'Well, I only have one condition——'

'Condition? It seems to me we've already been through all that.'

'——which is, that you take me with you. As an adjunct, if I can't get on the team, but don't forget, I have some relevant skills of my own.'

She bit back a smile as she watched him digest her words. 'But, Jenny——'

'And weren't you just telling me it isn't so dangerous?'

Checkmated, he looked at her with chagrin. Then he laughed.

'OK, it's a deal. For now. Later, we can renegotiate the contract.' Looking inordinately pleased with this strictly unilateral agreement, he drew her back into his arms.

'Renegotiate?' she asked, trying to wriggle free. 'Why should we renegotiate?'

He laughed and held her all the more firmly. 'Well, I was thinking it was about time we started giving serious thought to the creation of Paul Conan Brant the Fourth,' he said, dipping his head to nuzzle at the lobe of her ear. 'Family tradition to maintain, you know.'

'But what does that have to do with——'

'Somebody's going to have to stay home and look after him.'

'And that somebody has to be *me*?' she retorted indignantly. 'What do you think this is, the nineteenth century? Honestly, you sound like a caveman——'

'Gr-r-r!' he said, and stopped her with a kiss. Then he pulled her body even closer to his, and bent his head to her throat, and not long after that Jenny decided that perhaps it was best to let the tomorrows take care of themselves.

The present was just too delicious.

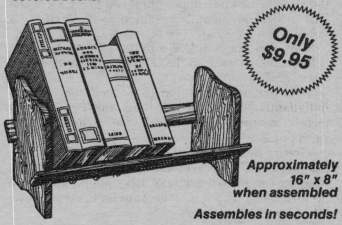

The passionate saga
that began with SARAH continues in the compelling,
unforgettable story of

Elizabeth

MAURA SEGER

In the aftermath of the Civil War, a divided nation—and two
tempestuous hearts—struggle to become one.

Harlequin Intrigue
Adopts a New Cover Story!

We are proud to present to you
the new Harlequin Intrigue cover design.

Look for two exciting new stories each month, which
mix a contemporary, sophisticated romance with the
surprising twists and turns of a puzzler . . . romance
with "something more."

Coming in April
Harlequin Category Romance Specials!

Look for six new and exciting titles from this mix of two genres.

4 Regencies—lighthearted romances set in England's Regency period (1811-1820)

2 Gothics—romance plus suspense, drama and adventure

Regencies

Daughters Four by Dixie Lee McKeone
She set out to matchmake for her sister, but reckoned without the Earl of Beresford's devilish sense of humor.

Contrary Lovers by Clarice Peters
A secret marriage contract bound her to the most interfering man she'd ever met!

Miss Dalrymple's Virtue by Margaret Westhaven
She needed a wealthy patron—and set out to buy one with the only thing she had of value....

The Parson's Pleasure by Patricia Wynn
Fate was cruel, showing her the ideal man, then making it impossible for her to have him....

Gothics

Shadow over Bright Star by Irene M. Pascoe
Did he want her shares to the silver mine, her love—or her life?

Secret at Orient Point by Patricia Werner
They seemed destined for tragedy despite the attraction between them....

CAT88A-1

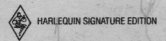

CAROLE MORTIMER

JUST ONE NIGHT

Hawk Sinclair—Texas millionaire and owner of the exclusive
Sinclair hotels, determined to protect his son's inheritance.
Leonie Spencer—desperate to protect her sister's happiness.

They were together for just one night.
The night their daughter was conceived.

Blackmail, kidnapping and attempted murder add suspense
to passion in this exciting bestseller.

The success story of Carole Mortimer continues with *Just
One Night*, a captivating romance from the author of the
bestselling novels, *Gypsy* and *Merlyn's Magic*.

★

**Available in March
wherever paperbacks are sold.**